The Voyage of the Sea Wolf

THE VOYAGE OF THE SEA WOLF

By Eve Bunting

PUBLISHED BY SLEEPING BEAR PRESS™

Copyright © 2012 Eve Bunting

Library of Congress Cataloging-in-Publication Data

Voyage of the Sea Wolf / by Eve Bunting.
p. cm.
Summary: After having been marooned on an island for ten days, Catherine and William are finally rescued and brought aboard a pirate ship that is captained by a woman who takes a liking to William and forbids Catherine, his true love, from seeing him.

[1. Pirates—Fiction. 2. Seafaring life—Fiction. 3. Love—Fiction.
4. Adventure and adventurers—Fiction.] I. Title.
PZ7.B91527Vo 2012
[Fic]—dc23   2011032089

ISBN 978-1-58536-789-4 (case)
10 9 8 7 6 5 4 3 2 1

ISBN 978-1-58536-790-0 (paperback)
10 9 8 7 6 5 4 3 2 1

This book was typeset in Adobe Caslon Pro and ITC Blackadder
Cover design by Richard Tuschman

Printed and bound in the United States.

Sleeping Bear Press˚

315 East Eisenhower Parkway, Suite 200
Ann Arbor, Michigan 48108

Sleeping Bear Press, a part of Cengage Learning.

visit us at www.sleepingbearpress.com

For Tracy Taylor Bunting

Chapter One

I stood with William, knee deep in the water, waving with all the strength I had left, at the brigantine anchored offshore.

"They're coming." William's hand tightened in mine.

A longboat was being lowered off the ship. Three men jumped into it and began pulling toward shore.

William and I leaned against each other. Even the little waves whispering around our feet had enough power to knock us over.

William whispered against my hair, "We are going to live, my love." His voice was cracked and almost inaudible.

I looked up into his face, the skin dry and burnt, the lips split and flaked with blood. My heart ached with love for him. We'd been so near to perishing on the island that one more day would have seen us dead in each other's arms. One more day.

The longboat was now only a half mile or so from shore. The morning was so still, so silent, that I could faintly hear the voices of the rowers and the small slaps of their oars against the water.

I moved a little apart from William and willed my voice to stay steady. "When they see that I am a girl they may not want to rescue me." I had to stop for the breath and strength to go on. "We know how seamen feel about having a woman on board. William, if that happens you must go without me. I could not bear..."

He touched a finger to my lips that were dry and sore as his own.

"Shh!" he whispered. "I'll never leave ye. Never."

Now the men on the longboat had shipped their oars and were drifting only a few yards from shore.

"Ahoy there!" one of them called. He was dark complected, his hair stringy and straight, bound back with a red scarf. For a moment I though he was a bandit, stepped from the pages of one of my childhood books. I blinked.

"Ahoy!" William croaked.

"We got our orders to pick yez up. Get yerselves out here and climb in if yez don't aim to be left behind."

"Could yez come a bit nearer," William began. "We..."

"This be's as far as we goes, matey."

"We can do it," I whispered, and clutching each other's hands we splashed through the shallows. My feet barely touched the bottom and I floundered, trying always to keep my precious flute above the surface. It was the only possession I had been allowed to bring with me when we were marooned by the *Reprisal*. The flute had saved our lives when I'd used it to signal the rescue ship. I was not going to let go of it now.

Once I stumbled, and William pulled me up. I was choking on the water I'd swallowed, coughing and spluttering.

"Get on me back," William ordered. "Put yer arms about my neck. If we sink we'll sink together."

"No." I could see that he was a poor swimmer. He was floundering, as I was. "I'll not weigh you down," I said.

We struggled together, the men watching as we splashed the last few feet to the boat.

I grabbed hold of the gunwale and one of them heaved me up the rest of the way. I fell, sodden and exhausted, at the rower's feet.

I lifted my head. "William?" I gasped. And then I

saw that he was already clambering over the gunwale, collapsing into the boat beside me.

"Are ye all right?" His hand reached out to touch me.

"Aye." I turned my head and retched, water spewing from my mouth, my empty stomach cramping on itself.

"What ship were yez put off?" the bandit asked.

"The *Reprisal*," William said.

"Were yez thieves, or cheaters or murderers that they set ye ashore? No matter." We got a stumpy-toothed smile. "How long was ye marooned?"

"Ten days," William said.

"That long? Yes did well." Then, "By heaven she be's a wench," he shouted. The other two stared. "Prop the girl up, Magruder," he called out and I was pulled to a place where I could lean against the wooden side of the boat. My flute had skittered across the boards. I crawled toward it and picked it up.

"Shiver me britches, look at the wench!" the one called Magruder said and for the first time I gave thought to how I must appear. So much had happened since my father had brought me on board his ship, disguised as a boy. There was no need to pretend anymore and now it would not be possible. On the island my clothes, little though they were, had torn and ripped. My trousers hung in tatters. I'd wrenched off the bottom of my shirt to make a bandage on the day that William had gashed his foot on a coral rock. Now it barely covered my bosom. I wrapped my arms across myself.

"Ye'd best leave her be," the rower at the back of the boat said. "Cap'n wants 'em brought and brought fast." This was the first time he'd spoken.

"Skelly's right." Bandit nodded.

"Wait!" Skelly pulled a waterskin from a pouch on his belt. He scrambled toward me, uncapped the skin and held the neck of it to my lips.

Water!

I sucked greedily, water trickling down my chin onto my chest, wasting itself on the bottom of the boat.

"Not too much to start," he said, pulling it away. " 'Twill make ye sick."

His small consideration made me feel less alone.

He crawled to William.

I watched William drink, spilling more than he could swallow.

"That's kindness enough, Skelly," Bandit said. "Get to the oars or I'll be tellin' Cap'n how 'twas ye that wasted our time."

Skelly pushed the stopper back in the waterskin. He was small and bald, the top of his head freckled and scarred from the sun. His black-rimmed eyeglasses were tied on his ears with cord. I tried to smile my gratitude at him as he sat on the bench again and took up his oars.

He did not smile back.

Magruder leaned across and touched my arm. "Soft!" he said.

"Do not touch me," I said firmly and he recoiled in mock horror.

"Leave her be," Bandit said. "We needs to get back."

They bent to the oars and the brigantine came closer and closer.

Dazed as I was, I still felt something amiss. The ship flew an English flag. But these sailors did not wear English sailor uniforms. Now I could see the name, scrolled in gold across the brigantine's side. *Sea Wolf.* I looked again at the English flag drooping from her mainmast. "We flies any flag that suits us," Red had told me once. He'd winked. Red, my only friend on the *Reprisal*, except for William. The *Sea Wolf* could be out of another country altogether. She might even be a privateer or a pirate vessel in disguise. Perhaps we had escaped from one ship of iniquity to be saved by another.

The men were rowing strongly now.

Magruder looked at me and puckered his lips in a kissing gesture.

I tried unsuccessfully to cover myself.

"By all that's holy we'll be glad to have ye on board the *Wolf*," he said. "I can't say aught for the cap'n."

What was he saying? Would the captain want to put me back, alone on the island? Me, a woman, bringing bad luck to his ship? Would he have left me there if he'd seen me to be female when he looked through his spyglass at the two of us, waving, my flute crying for help? I understood nothing but I was cold, cold, cold and filled with fear. The decision to take me or leave me could be put to a vote. My fate would depend on the crew.

When I looked beyond Magruder now I could see the *Sea Wolf* close up. She was beautiful, the kind of ship I'd dreamed of when I'd been longing to go to sea. A mermaid figurehead, green and golden, thrust her garlanded bosom out to the sea ahead. I thought of the red dragon on the *Reprisal*'s bow, then turned painfully to where Pox Island was growing smaller and smaller behind us. Now it seemed I had been happy there, happy with William and the love we'd found. I stretched out a hand to touch his hair as yellow as the day I'd first seen him on the beach at Cannon Cove. He'd been helping to provision the *Reprisal* for her journey and the golden gleam of that hair in the sun had taken my eye. The cabin boy, they'd told me.

He seemed to feel my light caress on his hair.

"Catherine," he whispered. "Whatever is ahead for us, we will face it together. Promise me that?"

"I promise," I whispered, though I knew our destiny, whether it be together or apart, would not be ours to decide.

Chapter Two

Towering over us, the *Sea Wolf* lay beautiful and serene in the blue waters of the Caribbean. Her deck railings were lined with men and there were two figures at the bow. The captain, maybe, and the quartermaster. A rope ladder hung over the side, dangling into our longboat that had been maneuvered under it.

"Get up and climb, young mistress," Bandit said. He held the bottom of the ladder while I stood, swaying with the motion of the longboat. Rung by rung I began to pull myself up.

"Set yer left foot first on the deck," Bandit shouted. "Cap'n be's superstitious. 'Tis bad luck to put yer right foot on the deck afore yer left 'un."

I had a back thought of the first day I'd climbed onto the deck of the *Reprisal*. My father, the ship's captain, had been already aboard. I remembered, as I climbed, how that first day, I'd been wearing the canvas shoes he'd bought for me, the way he'd cut the toes out of them with his cutlass when he'd discovered he'd bought them a size too small. He'd bought me the canvas trousers that I still wore, torn now and ragged. He'd bought me everything to wear that would disguise me as a boy and allow him to take me aboard his ship.

I clung to the rope ladder, racked with pain that was physical and spiritual, too. If only it were my father I was going to now, my father's ship, my father's loving presence. My own dear father, dead while trying to save me from the cat-o'-nine-tails.

There was a wind, one of the quick sudden wind bursts that blow up on the Caribbean. I clung tight to the ropes under my hands.

"Hurry along," Magruder yelled from below. I heard the impatience in his voice and he gave the rope ladder a jiggle so that I had to steady myself with my bleeding feet against the side of the ship. My flute, which I had pushed into the torn band of my trousers, poked my stomach and scraped against the hull.

I clenched my teeth and began climbing again.

I was more than halfway up and the men on the deck had started to catcall and shout what might have been encouragement.

"Pull harder, matey!"

"Show a bit o' muscle. Ye climb like a sick crab."

They called words unintelligible, blown away on the wind, and leaned across the railing, urging me on. One of them spat, the glob missing me and hitting Magruder or Bandit or Skelly below. Whoever it was let out a howl.

The ladder swung away from the hull and back again, almost forcing me to lose my grip. I felt the extra weight on it, the sharp tug, and when I looked below I saw the top of William's head. He had started up.

I had such a need then to climb down again, to be with him. We could jump into the ocean and swim for a while, then drown together.

"Don't be lookin' back, love," William shouted. "Keep on lookin' up."

I kept climbing.

They hadn't made me for a girl yet, but I had two more rungs to go before I was over the top. And what then?

Hands grabbed me and lifted me over to belly flop on the deck.

I felt the unbelieving stares of a hundred eyes.

"She be's a girl," a man yelled at last. "Cap'n. She be's a female."

There was a hubbub of voices and someone grabbed my torn shirt and ripped it off me. I pressed my naked self against the boards of the deck.

"Oh, aye, she be's a female!"

"I can see that."

"Step back, all of you!"

Heads turned to that voice. There was the shuffle of reluctant feet sliding away from me.

The wind had eased now and the forceful voice came to me clearly. "Jenks, take off that putrid rag of a shirt you're wearing and give it to her."

I lay, dazed, not believing what I was hearing. It was a woman's voice that had given the order. A voice of authority but distinctly female. The captain was a woman!

"Aye aye, Cap'n," the man, maybe Jenks, said and a foul-smelling shirt was dropped on my back. I wriggled into it and pulled it around me before I tried to get up. It fell to cover my exposed bosoms and stomach and the flute, still safe in what was left of the band on my trousers.

"Help her, you nincompoops. Help her up and then stand away," the woman shouted.

"I'm able myself," I said and struggled to my feet.

For the first time I saw her.

She was tall, so tall, and her hair was a red bush that circled her head, as big around as the wheel of a small cart. Her eyes were fixed on me with curiosity but I saw no vile intent in them. Her costume was that of any sailor, a loose striped shirt and bagging trousers. I saw the sharp edge of a cutlass dragging just below the hem of the shirt.

"Captain," I said in a voice as strong as I could make it. "Thank you for saving us."

William was beside me now. "Are ye all right?" His arm circled my shivering shoulders.

"Aye," I whispered.

"Who have we here?" the captain asked. "Did ye put yer correct foot on my deck, ye lubber?"

William didn't answer.

She was staring at him now and I heard the loud intake of her breath and saw her reach out toward him then pull her hand back. All she said was, "Who are you?"

"I am William. I was cabin boy on the pirate ship *Reprisal.*"

The captain slapped the shoulder of the man beside her whom I took to be the quartermaster. "The *Reprisal* is it, ahead o' us? I was right in my surmising. It was worth our time to pick them up."

Bandit took a step forward. "We hurried them back to ye, Cap'n." The servility in his voice made me cringe.

I had recovered enough now to really look at her. I'd never seen anyone like her. She was one of those Amazon women I had read about, a race of warrior women in ancient Greece, so big and ruthless that all were afraid of them. This Amazon was taller than any woman I had ever seen and broad of shoulder. Her red hair gave off sparks and her eyes... they were RED. Red eyes. It could not be true! Who was she, this captain with the red hair and the red eyes, a woman so fierce and dominant that a ship filled with seamen did her bidding? A ship filled with pirates, for already I knew that was what they were. They crowded around us, watching and listening.

"Cook," the captain called and a swarthy man stepped forward. "Yes, Cap'n?"

"Bring water and two dishes of that hen soup we had last night for our guests. Be sure there's meat in it. Make haste." She spoke her orders but I noticed her eyes were always on William. It made me uneasy.

But the thought of food was overpowering.

Saliva spurted into my mouth. Hen soup! Water! My thirst was suddenly so strong that my whole body shook.

"Now, the rest of you, you lazy stinking dogs, get this ship underway. We'll need to catch up with the *Reprisal* before she comes upon the *Isabella*. Mr. Forthinggale! You stay here."

"Aye, Cap'n."

There was a scurrying, a rush of men to the masts, voices calling orders. Lines were loosed. I heard the grating heavy scrape of a chain and realized the anchor was being raised.

I stood, stunned. She was after the *Reprisal*! I'd never thought to see that ship again. The deck, stained with my father's blood. Hopper and Herc who had marooned us.

Mr. Forthinggale stood by the captain. The remembrance of Mr. Trimble, quartermaster on the *Reprisal*, came to me. Mr. Trimble, quartermaster and friend to my father. Mr. Trimble who had betrayed me. I brought my mind back quickly for the Amazon captain was addressing me.

"You!"

William's arm tightened around me.

"Leave go of her, William," the captain said. "She be's a woman. She can stand on her own. How are you called?" she asked me.

William's grip did not loosen.

Under that red, angry stare he stood firm.

I spoke at once before the captain could scream or slash at him.

"My name is Catherine DeVault. My father was Captain DeVault, of the ship *Reprisal*." I let myself slide down to sit with my back to the railing.

Under us I felt the deck sway, and when I looked up I saw that the sails were already spread and the *Sea Wolf* was moving.

"I am Captain Medb Moriarity, captain and owner of the *Sea Wolf*," she said. "My father built this ship. Now she is mine."

The words came from me before I could stop them. "Medb? You were called after the daughter of the High King of Ireland?

The captain's eyes widened. "You know of her?"

"Yes," I said. "The most renowned warrior. I have admired her." I repeated the name. "Medb. I had not known the right pronunciation. Medb, which sounds like 'seed.' I have read of her exploits."

She nodded. "So you have learning?"

"Yes, Captain." I realized I was feeling dizzy and that the deck and the sky were turning circles in my mind. I blinked hard.

"How came ye to be marooned?" Captain Medb Moriarity asked.

I mustered the strength to answer, "When they found me to be female, they..."

The cook placed a bowl of water and another of soup in front of me and handed the same to William.

The smell wafted up to me and my eyes teared with

anticipation. I took a long, sweet draught of water then grabbed the bowl. Grease beaded the top. There were potatoes in the soup and green leafy vegetables of some kind and a hen's yellow foot. It kept bumping against my teeth as I drank. I felt strength coming back to me with each deep swallow.

The captain stood, watching.

When I'd drained every drop I picked up the hen's foot, and gnawed and sucked on its gristle.

William took the hen's foot from his own bowl and reached it to me.

"None of that," the captain said. "You eat! She has had her share."

"And I choose to give her my share," William said and in an instant the captain stepped forward, grabbed the hen's foot that was still in his hand and flung it over the side into the water.

"Next time, do as I tell you," she said.

William shrugged. "Aye, aye, Cap'n." His tone was insolent and I knew to be insolent with this woman would be a mistake. I waited for her rage and it came in the flare of her red eyes and the instinctive way her hand dropped to her cutlass.

She stood for a moment then said, "Careful, William. I may not always be this patient with you."

I saw her look up then and I looked too.

There was the thump of wind in the sails and I could hear the hiss of the sea against the hull.

The *Sea Wolf* was underway.

I wondered what was in store for William and me now.

Chapter Three

The ship was moving well.

Captain Moriarity looked from one of us to the other.

"So Mistress Catherine, they put you off because you're a woman. Or almost a woman," the captain said and it was as if the hen's foot scene had not happened. "Bad cess to them for a band of mangy dogs. Most men are mangy dogs. I've known some."

Mr. Forthinggale, who had stood quiet behind her, scowled.

She looked at me. "How far ahead would the *Reprisal* be?"

"Ten days at the least," I answered. "But she had two of her timbers smashed below the waterline. I heard Herc say they would be pulling her out for repairs on Mutiny Island. Herc is captain now in my father's place."

The captain's eyes narrowed. "Repairs will take up some of her time. Did the cap'n speak of the *Isabella*?"

"No," William said.

The captain nodded. "She's not on that course then. She'll take her time." She squinted at the sparkling ocean. "Does she carry a goodly booty? The *Reprisal*?"

"Aye. She raided two ships since we left Port Teresa." I had no feeling of disloyalty to my father's old ship and its new captain. Bad cess to them.

"How many guns does she sport?"

"Four," William said.

Her smile was wolfish. "We carry ten, and eighty crew, all o' them sons o' the *Sea Wolf*, all willin' to shed their blood for a treasure. 'Twill be worth making a small stop on our way to our prize. My crew has need of a diversion."

Her appraising gaze rested on William and again I felt that nervous twitch inside me. What were her thoughts? I wondered. What was her obvious interest in him?

I watched him, too: so tall and strong, the cuts on his back healed to white stripes, his skin dark and smooth from sea and sun, his face with its trace of a scar, his eyes, blue as the sea, that shock of yellow hair. In that instant I remembered how we had held each other as we lay on the beach of Pox Island. A shiver coursed through me.

The captain was still staring at him. Her eyes, I now saw, were not red. They were a dark brown that seemed to hold a redness in their depths, like the brandy my father used to drink with Mr. Trimble. Sometimes they would hold their glasses up to the light in a toast to the *Reprisal* or to the new voyage and the brandy inside was the color of leaves in autumn. Perhaps it was the reflection of the captain's mass of red hair that I had seen mirrored in her eyes before.

"Have you used a cutlass? A knife?" she asked William. "Are you adept with the cannon?"

"Aye, Captain," he replied.

"I can wield such weapons, too," I said. "I can fight if there's something to fight for."

The captain nodded. "What work did you do on the *Reprisal*?"

"I played flute with the ship's musicians," I said. "It was my flute shining that drew you to Pox Island." I lifted the hem of the grimy shirt that covered me to show it to her.

"Flute?" she asked. "Ship's musicians? Snake's tooth! What kind of a ship was it with nothing to do but listen to music?"

"We played to frighten the enemy. Wavering, they called it. Do not be misled, Captain Moriarity. It was not all music when the *Reprisal* did battle. I was part of the combat."

She nodded. "I've heard of this wavering." She laughed then, a rollicking belly laugh. Behind her Mr. Forthinggale tittered. "Me, I'm content to slaughter my enemies." Her arm sliced back and forth in front of her, brandishing an imaginary cutlass.

She moved toward me and stared, as though evaluating me. "Catherine? Did you and William..." She paused. "Did you become affectionate with each other? There on that island?"

I pulled the foul-smelling shirt tightly around me and stood straight, not allowing myself to tremble at the sudden sharpness of her voice.

"Yes," I said.

"Ask yer questions of me," William said. "Let her be."

"I address whom I please," she said coldly. "There'll be none o' that affection on my ship. None! I don't hold with it. And there'll be no chance meetings between the two of yez either."

She leaned toward me. "There're islands between here and where we're headed," she said. "You want to be marooned again? I'll put ye off if I hear a babble about the two of you. And it'll be a different island for each. Ye'll be alone. Think on that, the two o' ye. Understand?"

"Yes," I said and William nodded.

Her face came close to mine. "There's Turtle Rock," she said. "Two days' sail from here."

Inside I quaked but I looked straight at her. I had a bargaining tool. A bargaining tool worth fighting for or killing for. The Burmese Sunrise! My father had died for that jewel. It was to be the start of life together for William and me. But I would tell her of it, if the time came to save William's life and mine. Not now. I had watched the pirates on the *Reprisal* playing cards and I knew enough to understand that you kept the strongest card in your hand till the end. You kept it hidden.

"Mr. Forthinggale!" the captain called.

The quartermaster stepped forward.

"Make it known to the crew that these two are never to speak to each other, never to touch. Do ye understand, Quartermaster?"

"Aye, Captain."

"Make sure the crew understand. They are to watch them. If they see or hear aught of them communicatin', they are to report to me. If not, there will be punishment for them too. And they are to leave the girl be. I want no fightin' over a wench on my vessel. Now, cut me off a piece of that yellow hair. And mind you don't cut his head along wi' it."

"Aye, Cap'n."

Mr. Forthinggale pulled a knife from his belt. "Don't ye move now, boy," he said and with one swoop he sliced off a goodly chunk of William's hair.

I couldn't prevent a small cry of distress.

The hair fell in a bright yellow clump on the deck. Wisps of it blew in the breeze, some drifting over into the ocean.

Mr. Forthinggale gathered up what was left on the deck and presented it to the captain.

Why did she want it? It could not be for sentimental reasons. Captain Moriarity was an old woman.

She stood for a moment, looking at the lock of hair, then said, "Mr. Forthinggale! Take the two of them to the clothes chest. Then bring them back on deck to take the oath."

"Aye, Cap'n."

I knew she meant the Code of Conduct that we would have to swear to and I wanted to say that we had already taken the oath on the *Reprisal*. But I knew that this was her ship and an old oath would not satisfy her.

Without another word she walked away.

William smiled down at me, that smile that melted my heart. He did not touch me or take my hand. Mr. Forthinggale was beside us but even he could not control

William's smile.

I watched Captain Medb Moriarty strut along the deck. She carried herself like a queen, as if she owned the ship and the world and everything in it.

I saw her look down at the clump of yellow hair she still held then slide it carefully into the pocket of her canvas trousers.

Chapter Four

We walked the deck, Mr. Forthinggale between us.

The pirates stopped their work as we passed and the faces turned toward us were dark and hostile. There were low mutterings and words that I could occasionally hear.

"Another woman on board."

"Bad fortune the day you picked her up, Bandit."

"There be's many a dark night with the sea waitin'," a tall, gangling pirate growled and spat on the deck.

I stopped and turned toward him. "The captain makes decisions on the ship," I said. "She has made her decision about me. It would not be wise to go against her."

William strode forward and grabbed his shoulder.

"You miserable cur," he said. "You touch one hair o' her head..."

Mr. Forthinggale jerked him back. "Ye'll answer to me afore ye answer to the captain, if'n ye harm her," he said. "They're here, the two of them. Captain's orders, if ye see them touching or hear them conversing you are to disclose it to her. And ye're to keep yer hands off the wench and yer remarks to yerselves. She is no plaything, brought on board for yer pleasure."

To me his words lacked conviction. I doubted if he would ever protect me should the need arise.

I saw Skelly, who'd given us water in the longship, and Magruder, who'd been there, too. My eyes lingered for a second on Magruder and he made that obscene kissing sound that was more horrifying to me than the spoken threats.

Right then I knew I would have to get a knife and keep it by me, awake or asleep.

Walking the length of the deck with Mr. Forthinggale I got my first real look at the *Sea Wolf*. She was beautiful, all polished wood and small embellishments. A golden horseshoe was nailed to the main mast. A carved oaken board hung above the door to the bridge. On it were etched the words Bonne Chance, which I knew to be French for "good luck." It had likely been on a pillaged

French ship. The railings shone. They were scarred and battle wounded but still they gleamed. I thought they might be made of oak also. There was no roughness in this ship, no shoddiness. Loving hands had made her and she had been valued.

Now she was under full sail, the wind making that brisk lapping sound as it spread the canvas. I heard the slap-snap of the flag, the lying English flag. The deck sloped, lifted itself, dropped with the motion of the ship so that I saw the whole sweep of sky and clouds and sea. The salt mist of spray filled my senses. If only this had been another time and another place, if this had been our ship, mine and William's, and we were off on a new adventure...

I reminded myself of what a miracle it was that he and I had been rescued from certain death and how fortunate that the ship had a woman captain. Had it been a man, he might have made a different judgment. She was a strange woman, but a woman. I sensed in her a mixture of lady and villain. But the way she had acted with William disturbed me greatly.

I had a flash of something like jealousy, which I told myself was absurd. The captain must be at least twenty-seven or twenty-eight years of age. It was possible that she found him handsome. Who would not? But to be jealous of her was foolish. I had enough to concern me.

Mr. Forthinggale held up his hand for us to stop. He kicked the side of a battered wooden chest that was pushed against a bulwark then lifted the lid with the toe of his boot. The chest was half-filled with clothing and the smell that wafted up from it told me it had been a long time since anything in it had been washed. The foul odors of sweat, urine, and old, stale whiskey or rum overpowered the clean smell of the salt air. Bile rose in my throat.

"Find what you need." Forthinggale made a disgusted face as he lifted an old torn shirt with the point of his knife and dropped it back on top of the filthy jumble inside.

"Here girl," he said then. "These were Frenchy's. He got tired o' them. They're high style and right for you." He waved a pair of green satin pantaloons like a flag and held them out to me. One glance told me they were almost clean and untorn. I took them off the knife's point and set them beside me.

"Find yerselves some shirts. Never get any cheaper," Forthinggale said with that high-pitched giggle that did not match his appearance.

William rustled through the chest and brought out some clothing that looked usable. As he shook out a faded flowered shirt, rat droppings fell from it in a soft patter on the deck. Mr. Forthinggale flattened them with his boot and ground them into the wood.

"Is there a place to wash these things?" I asked him.

He shrugged. "There's a bucket below decks. Ye can draw up some water."

William examined a sweat-stained white shirt then pulled it on.

The shirt was small. He was thin from the island but still it strained against his shoulders. I watched him roll up the sleeves, the small golden hairs on his arms glinting in the sun.

"Who wore this clothing afore us?" he asked.

"The crew." Mr. Forthinggale's voice was disinterested. "When we takes over another ship the men seize the captives' garments, if they're any better than their own. That's afore they cuts their throats. Come on."

He turned and William and I secretly touched hands before we bundled the clothes and followed him.

The wind was in front of us, the deck alive with activity. No one turned as we walked past. Backs were bent, hands were busy.

Then I saw why.

Captain Medb Moriarity leaned against a coil of rope, deep in conversation with the smallest man I'd ever seen in my life. He had a shock of black hair that curled out from under a red kerchief and his top half was sturdy and strong looking. But his legs were short and stubby as a small child's. I had never seen a dwarf before but I knew this pirate to be one. Neither of them looked at us as we passed and the captain made no answer to Mr. Forthinggale's polite "Captain?"

The man was speaking.

"One only," he said. His voice was low and I began to wonder if I'd interpreted his words correctly.

"How was it?" the captain asked.

"Empty."

The captain breathed hard. "Empty? That is not good. She has come out then? She is here. Could she be the girl?"

The dwarf looked up at me and narrowed his eyes.

"Step forward, Catherine," the captain ordered.

I took a pace forward. What was this? Panic choked my throat. What had she meant when she asked, "Could she be the girl?"

The dwarf stood in front of me, his little legs planted apart.

"Cap'n," William began and the captain held up a hand and hissed. "Be quiet."

I stood still, enduring the steady gaze of the little man. I tried to think of other things but my mind was strangely blank.

After what seemed forever he shook his head and moved back.

"Ye have no need to worry, Cap'n. Not on this account."

The captain indicated for me to step back.

"Captain?" Mr. Forthinggale asked, timidly I thought.

The captain swung around. "What is it? You know better than to interrupt me when I'm speakin' wi' Sebastian."

"Aye, Captain. I just want to ask if ye'll be giving the oath right away. Or are the marooners to be cleaned up first?"

The dwarf, Sebastian, examined his fingers, sucking on one of them.

"They'll take the oath the way they are." The captain's voice was calmer. "I apologize for my rudeness, Mr. Forthinggale. You know I am not always on line with the horizon when I am in discussion with Sebastian." Her head inclined toward us. "Sebastian, these are Catherine and William."

When she said William's name it seemed to me her whole manner softened, became boneless, the way a cat's does when it sleeps. I was fancying it, I knew. And then I saw her gently touch the pocket of her trousers where I'd earlier seen her slip the cutting of his hair.

I bit my lip. No, I was not fancying anything.

Chapter Five

r. Forthinggale held a sheet of paper. He indicated to me to sit on the cannon nearest to him. I set my bundle of clothes on the deck.

Standing by the railing was the dwarf, Sebastian. His gaze on me was steady as it had been when he had examined me for the captain and made that strange pronouncement, "Ye have no need to worry. Not on this account." What did it mean?

"Should I administer the oath to the both of them together?" Mr. Forthinggale asked the captain. "It would save time."

The captain glared. "Have ye not hearkened to me?

There's to be nothin' for them together. Did I not make myself clear?"

"Aye, Captain." Mr. Forthinggale's face turned an unbecoming shade of red.

I thought how strange it was that this bullying, unpleasant man should be cowed by her. It was an indication to me of her strength that she could so easily intimidate him and the rest of the crew. Perhaps not Sebastian. With him she had been even respectful.

I straddled the cold metal of the cannon. My tattered trousers left my legs almost bare, torn as they were from waist to ankle. I saw the looks and nudges of the men who had gathered to listen and I tried to arrange the tattered trousers like a long skirt to better cover me.

I smiled reassurance at William who stood to the side.

Mr. Forthinggale cleared his throat and began.

The Code of Conduct was almost the same as the one I had taken on my father's ship.

I was not to gamble at cards or dice. The crew of the *Reprisal* had been bound by the same order but they had gambled ferociously, even on the rats that they brought up from the bilges.

I was not to have a candle lighted after eight at night for fear of fire.

I was not to strike another member of the crew while

aboard the *Sea Wolf.*

"Hear that, Skull?" someone shouted. "Ye should be put in irons for what ye did to me."

"Shut yer mouth! Ye started it."

There was a small scuffle, quickly subdued.

My mind wandered back to the way it had been on the *Reprisal* when it had been my father's voice reading the conditions of the Code. There had been the one provision in his that was not included here. The one that stated that the musicians were on duty every day except for Sundays. Captain Moriarity had no time for music.

As Mr. Forthinggale continued, telling how the shares of plunder would be divided, I found myself wondering why the captain herself did not administer the oath. As captain, I thought, it should be her business, not the quartermaster's. And then I thought, she considers herself Medb, who was born daughter to the High King of Ireland and who herself became Queen of Connacht. She had peasants to do her bidding. Captain Medb had peasants to do *her* bidding. Their names were pirates.

I listened as the quartermaster's voice droned on.

The day was lovely, filled with sunshine and sea. Small clouds bubbled in the sky. The sails were bursting with wind and, even though I was in danger, I felt in that moment happy to be alive, to be here, to be able to look across and see my love, my William.

When the ceremony came to an end I climbed carefully off the cannon, mindful of some modesty, and signed my name to the papers. Catherine DeVault. For better or worse I was now a crewmember on the *Sea Wolf*.

William took the same oath after me. I had wondered if the captain would let me stay to see him and I tried to make myself small as I stood a little apart, hoping she would not notice me.

I watched as he signed the Code. There would be only William written on the paper. No last name. He had never had one.

"Men! All is over." The captain made a dismissal signal with her arms. "William, you go with them. Ye'll do what's needed, scrub decks, empty the bilges, check the cannons. Ye'll sleep wi' the crew. Get a hammock if there is one or find a place for yerself on the fo'c's'le though the men are stuck together there like salt fish in a barrel."

"Pork can squeeze hisself a bit," someone yelled. "He's such'n a fat pig he takes up two places."

There was much laughter and punching. Like the pirates on the *Reprisal* this was a companionship of ruffians and if you didn't know better you would think them all jolly and fun loving. They were, when it suited them. But underneath they were thieves and murderers and scum.

William was following them but he stopped and turned when the captain addressed me.

"Cate," the captain began.

"Her name is Catherine," William called back.

"She'll be Cate on my ship." The captain's voice was harsh and angry. "Ye'll not be callin' her with any name nor talkin' to her neither. So ye have no need to worry."

"Then she'll be Catherine in my thoughts," William said. "And there'll be plenty of them, you can lay to that."

I touched a finger to my lips.

"There'll be none o' that neither," the captain said. There was fury in her face.

None o' that.

But I would be in his thoughts and even Queen Medb could not take those away.

"Cate! Sebastian is sail master on the *Sea Wolf*. He has asked that ye work with him on the sails. 'Tis an important task. Ye'll be busy on them from mornin' to sunset and Sebastian will be keeping a watch on ye. Ye'll take yer orders from him. Ye're to sleep in my cabin. And I'll be watching ye there. So any notion ye might have on sneakin' away to William, put it out of yer mind. Do ye understand? You'd better!"

"I understand." I swallowed hard. My stomach was roiling a little, perhaps from the strangeness of the situation or perhaps from the hen soup.

"I have washing water there and a commode," the captain continued. "Ye can use the washing water after me if you have a mind to. Not before. And never use the commode. I do not wish what comes out of you to mix with what comes out o' me."

"Aye, Captain." I wanted to ask where I should go when I needed to relieve myself but it did not seem appropriate. No doubt I would find out for myself.

Sebastian had stood listening and watching. She did not order him away.

Mr. Forthinggale, on Captain's orders, directed me to her cabin. He strode beside me and his expression was grim. I noticed that the turkey redness had gone from his face but he was still angry. He walked too fast so that I had to run to keep up. My stomach, so long without food, was cramping now so I moved half bent over.

We went down a set of stairs, turned toward the stern and stopped at an open door. "A captain's door must always be left open," my father had told me. "The crew can come and go as they please." It had been that way on the *Reprisal* and it seemed it was that way here. Would it be left open through the dark hours of night? If it was...?

"Get yerself settled," the quartermaster said in a surly voice. "Then get topside. Sebastian will be waiting for ye."

I dropped my bundle of clothing.

"Mr. Forthinggale?" My voice shook. "Quartermaster... I cannot. I feel deathly sick. 'Twas the soup I—" With that it all came rushing up, out of my stomach, down my nose, into my mouth. I had no control over it as it gushed out, over the captain's floor, over Mr. Forthinggale's booted feet.

He gave a little high-pitched squeal of disgust. Then the words spurted from him the way the vomit had spurted from me.

"Ye wretched, putrefying besom! Look at me boots! I'll never get the stink out. And captain's cabin! Do ye know what ye've done ye wretched, filthy dog?"

"It could not be helped," I said, wiping my mouth with the back of my hand. My stomach felt better. How had my bundle of clothing fared? Thankfully it was out of reach of my indelicate incident. But on the floor was a slimy puddle of yellow vomit. Mixed with the liquid I thought I saw some remnants of the hen's foot.

If my teacher with her emphasis on teaching me good manners could see me now!

"You'd best stay where ye are. I will inform the captain and Sebastian that you are unwell. 'Twill not get ye out of work, mind. We will see what Cap'n says. And get this cleaned up. Now. Before she has to look at it or smell it."

I was glad to see him go.

But how was I to clean it up?

I looked around the cabin.

It was as austere as my father's had been. There was a bunk with a gray blanket and a sturdy wooden chair bolted to the floor. Its high back and wide armrests gave it the look of a throne. There was a row of books on a shelf that had been slotted so they would stay in place even in a storm.

No time to inspect them now. I had to clean up the disgusting mess before Captain Moriarity saw it.

Against the wall was a wooden table, on it a water jug and basin, set into holders that were strapped down. I was never to use this before her. But now I had to. I loosened the straps, poured water into the basin, took a shirt that was no more than a rag from my bundle and washed the floor. It was slippery and nasty enough to make me sick all over again. But I could not afford to be delicate. Hard to believe this revolting accumulation had been in my stomach. And that it had tasted so good going down.

I carried the basin carefully from the cabin, up the stairs and onto the deck.

The cool evening air smelled of the sea, of tar and rope

and all things clean. I took long breaths, then went slowly to the rail and tipped what I had disgorged into the sea. The scum of it drifted on the surface, then sank. I tossed the ragged shirt after it. Then I went back to the cabin, rinsed out the basin, made another trip to the railing to empty the water and carried it back.

The quartermaster had ordered me to stay here.

I looked around the cabin.

The bed, the chair, the books.

The books! I went closer to read their titles. Many were on seafaring. Some were novels. I saw *Gulliver's Travels* and *The Tale of the Tub*. And then I saw a slim, small copy of *The Tain*. I knew it to be Ireland's greatest epic, the tale of Queen Medb and the brown bull of Cualinge. Captain Medb Moriarity's namesake. Had her father named her after the great Irish queen? Or had she named herself? I was tempted to look through it again but someone could come at any minute through that open door.

On the shelf next to the books was a small, carved box with an ivory lid. I wanted to open it but it had an air of secrecy about it, of value. My hand hovered above the lid. And then I knew. I knew what was in there and why I felt as I did. I lifted the lid, just enough, and saw the lock of William's hair, shining and golden. I lifted it out, touched it to my lips, then placed it carefully back in the box.

What had been bleak was even bleaker now.

I stumbled across the cabin calming myself. I was aware she had taken it, now I had discovered that she had kept it. What else did I expect? I must not let the knowledge unsettle me.

I looked around. In the corner beside the jug and washbasin was the porcelain commode with a wooden lid. A not-very-clean towel was suspended on a roller device. There was no hairbrush. My father's, the one my mother had given him, had been left on the *Reprisal* when Herc had thrown us off the ship.

I saw a sea chest, the lid closed tight with a lock and chain. Did Medb have other secrets in there? Most people had secrets that they kept hidden. I had a quick thought of the Burmese Sunrise—my secret, mine and William's— safely hidden in my mother's bedroom back in Port Teresa. Some day, I thought. Some day we will take it and use it and be together forever. And there will be no more Captain Moriarity.

There was a long cupboard, the kind that had been in my father's cabin. His had been big enough for me to hide in. I went across to this one and swung open the door. In it on a row of pegs hung several pieces of rough clothing and a dark-blue velvet jacket with gold braid, which I thought must be Captain Moriarity's "going to shore" apparel. There were blue velvet trousers, buckled at the knees, and on the shelf above were white silk stockings and shining black shoes with pointed toes. I imagined Captain Medb Moriarity stepping proudly through some exotic town, her red hair asparkle, her shining black shoes clattering on the cobblestones. So fashionable, so important. Queen of that town, too.

I got my bundle of clothes, stepped into the cupboard which was not as capacious as my father's but served well enough, discarded my own wretched trousers and pulled on the green pantaloons. They smelled of mildew and stale brandy but they could have been worse.

I tucked my flute into the waistband, patted it gently and whispered, "I still have you, my dear friend." It shamed me to feel tears behind my eyes.

As I stepped out again into the cabin I remembered how I had found my mother's silk petticoat in my father's cupboard. The memory bruised me. My beloved parents, both gone. My father's body somewhere in this big wide ocean, my mother's underneath the earth of Cobb Hill. Was the piece of pink coral my father had placed on her coffin still there?

My stomach had settled into an empty ache. The wet on the floor was drying. There was no trace left of my unfortunate accident.

The quartermaster had told me to stay here but I could not. Instead I would go back on deck and face the captain. And Sebastian.

Chapter Six

It was not easy to find my way back. The brigantine was unlike my father's ship. I knew we had come down steps and veered either left or right but I had lost sense of direction. I took several wrong turnings. Here was a set of steps leading down to the hold below decks. Animal sounds came up to me. I heard goats bleating and I thought of Daisy and Pansy, my goat friends on the *Reprisal*.

I went down holding on to the bulwarks on either side as the ship rolled beneath me.

There were three pens: one with a lone pig, one with two goats and one with four fat turtles. I thought the noise increased when they saw me. "Are ye begging to be set free?" I whispered. "If I could I would. But I'm a captive myself." I reached over and patted the head of one of the goats. I would not give her, or the other one, names. It would make it too easy to hold them dear and too difficult if you had to see them cut up and served in Salmagundi.

Chickens clucked inside both pens and pecked at the droppings and each other. I'd had chicken soup. I'd had the foot of one. The thought did not sit well.

I passed the hold where barrels of grain and flour and salt were strapped down and overflowing. Something moved behind one of the spilled barrels and I saw a sleek black cat. It looked at me with hostile eyes and I hurried by. I passed rolled up sails and coils of rope and the spare wood that all sailing ships carried in case of a mast needing to be replaced or a hull needing patched. This would be where the weapons were kept, probably in the locked chests that were lashed down in preparation for rough seas. Casks of water or wine or rum, dozens of them, lay side by side in a neat row. There was the musty smell of grain and animals and rancid bilge water. It was close and airless, hard to breathe. The brig was down here somewhere, dark and fetid and waiting. The brig! The sea, pushed against the hull, thumping like drumbeats. Like my heart.

I rushed back to the steps and ran up them.

Wind billowed my green satin pantaloons and drove

me forward. I took great gulps of the clean, salt air.

Crewmen rushed about the deck. One, whose name I did not yet know and who was carrying a small crate of limes, said, "Hey! Them's Frenchy's pantaloons. They looks better on you."

"Ye'd look more fetchin' without them, I'll lay to that," another one, fat and cumbersome, remarked.

"If I took them off I'd not be giving them to you then, Pork," I said. "You're too stout to fit into them." I did not know if he was the one they had called Pork or not. He fitted the description.

"Ye hear, Gabby?" Pork sounded pleased. "She knows me name!"

I scanned the deck for a glimpse of William but didn't find him. And then I saw Skelly. He sidled up to me. Sunlight dazzled on his glasses and I could not see his eyes. His bald head was hard and brown as a chestnut and freckled. "Pay a mind to Sebastian. He has much to tell and he likes to talk," he whispered. "But be wary. He has Captain's ear."

I nodded. I had already surmised that.

His thumb directed me. "He be's farther along there."

Sebastian sat on the deck surrounded by the billowing mass of a sail, the edge of which lay across his lap. I thought it must be the big, square-rigged sail off the foremast, but when I looked up I saw the wide squareness of it, still flying, blown full and swollen against the deepening blue of the sky. A spare sail then, perhaps the mizzen top gallant.

From this angle, his little legs hidden by the canvas, Sebastian looked like a full-sized man. His head was bigger than most, his hair hidden now under a dark-blue woolen cap.

He glanced up at me, grunted and indicated for me to sit next to him. I noticed that on one hand was a leather glove that wrapped around his wrist and palm with a hole for his fingers and thumb.

Below us the ship rocked back and forth. Spray misted my face, scattered by the push of the *Sea Wolf* through the waves.

"Take yerself one o' them needles," Sebastian said, pointing at a bundle that lay beside him.

I opened it. Inside was a row of needles, big as carpenters' nails. Next to them was a roll of brown string.

I stared at the needles and string, then at him. He was using one of the oversized needles as he worked.

"Did ye ever sew?" he asked, not looking at me but at

the sail he was mending. I saw that he poked the point of the needle at the canvas, then used the leather-protected pad on his palm to push it through the stiff sailcloth.

"I sewed a bit," I said. "Miss Grayson, my teacher, thought all young ladies should be adept at needlework. We made pinafores and skirts that we donated to women's charities. I hated it. I did not wish to be the kind of young lady that grows up to make samplers and embroiders handkerchiefs."

Why was I prattling on like this? Perhaps people did give Sebastian information about themselves and that was how he knew everything.

"What did ye want to be?"

His eyes were the deep green of the ocean close to shore. There was a quality to them that I had never before been aware of. They were listening eyes.

"A pirate," I said.

He studied me, sucking on his fingers. Now I could see why he did. The palm of his hand was protected but drops of blood speckled his fingertips. He licked them off.

I felt myself cringe.

"And what do ye want now?"

"To be free and with William," I said.

"Ye'll have to chart a course through dangerous waters afore that happens," he said.

I could not look away from the green of his eyes.

"Choose yerself a needle and start," he said at last. "We needs to get that rip there stitched."

I sat cross-legged beside him and chose a needle. Its eye was as big as a pea. He pointed to a knife and then at the string. I sawed myself off a length. It was coarse and hairy and tough, and I supposed it to be made from hemp ropes, the strands separated.

I started where the rip began, pushing the needle into the sailcloth, pushing and thrusting with all my strength before the point went through.

"Here." From under his edge of sail Sebastian produced another leather glove. "Put on this 'palm.' Ye'll not find the task as easy as makin' pinafores."

I was trying to use what Miss Grayson had taught as a running stitch, basting torn edge to torn edge.

"That'll not hold," Sebastian said. "One wallop of wind and it'll tear apart again. Ye have to whip yer stitches, like this."

He showed me what he had done. "Whip 'em over and over and over, so it'll stay bound."

I nodded. One inch and my fingers ached. The leather helped, but still I felt the metal of the needle eye dig into my hand. The muscles in my arm throbbed.

I didn't know how many minutes had passed when

Sebastian said, "It's raw work, girl, but it needs done."

I looked at my fingers. There was no blood, not yet, but already they were bruised and squashed. Tears stung my eyes. I was glad William could not see me, his brave girl, sniveling like a spoiled child. I cut myself a new length of the rope string, attached it to the needle and whipped and whipped and whipped. I reminded myself that this was nothing compared to starving to death on a barren rock island. But there was Turtle Rock and other islands where I could be put ashore again. And on Pox Island I had been with William.

A course to chart and dangerous waters.

I took a second to lick away the first drop of blood on my finger, then started again.

I must work. I must please Sebastian—Sebastian who had the captain's ear.

The captain must not deem me worthless. Always, always, Turtle Island shadowed my thoughts.

Chapter Seven

The sun was dropping toward the ocean. The sky was red as fire, shot through with streaks of palest pink. It was beautiful, but I had no time to admire it. Needle point in, push with the "palm," pull it through, yanking and struggling till the thread came after it.

Men spoke to us, or rather to Sebastian in passing. Small wonder he knew everything. I caught whispered words. They told Sebastian their woes or their quarrels, the pain in their feet, arms, guts. Sometimes they shared something amusing that made Sebastian laugh. Not for an instant did Sebastian's needle halt. He sewed and listened and briefly spoke.

Bare feet, dirty and calloused, and legs in frayed trousers filled my line of vision. How I wished William would walk by so I could get a glimpse of him, even just his feet. But wherever he had been given a job to do it was at the other end of the ship.

Mr. Forthinggale came, stopped and said to Sebastian, "I see the wench has recovered. Is she of any use to ye?"

"Aye," Sebastian said. "She is working rightly."

"Humph!" Mr. Forthinggale moved on.

A pirate with red shiny corns on his toes jeered, "If ye tire o' her Sebastian, I can keep her busy."

"Shut yer mouth, Puce," Sebastian said pleasantly, without looking up.

We both looked up when Captain Moriarity appeared.

I was prepared by Sebastian's order, "Cap'n be's comin'. Leave be wi' the needle and pay her attention."

"Aye." I gratefully set down my needle and found myself sucking my fingers as Sebastian had done. My stomach grumbled and though I had been sick I felt the need of food. There would be some sort of night meal. Perhaps I would have a chance to see William.

Captain Moriarity stopped in front of us. "Cate!" she said. "I see you're settling in. Don't be gettin' too comfortable. Lives change."

"I know that, Captain," I said. "And I would not call

what I am doing comfortable."

"Are ye being impudent?"

"No, Captain. Just telling what's true." Careful, Catherine, I warned myself. Do not be impudent with the captain. I stretched out one leg and rubbed it with my "palm."

She watched quizzically but said no more to me.

"Sebastian? Ye've seen naught?"

"No, Cap'n."

She nodded. "I will muster the crew on deck. I want you to inspect them. Be careful. There could be much at stake."

"Aye, Cap'n. If'n ye think it necessary."

"It is."

She made her imperious way along the deck and Sebastian sighed. He stood up and stretched.

"Ye can get in a line with the others though I've cleared ye already," he told me.

"Can I ask what this is about?" I said.

"Ye can ask. But I have no time to answer ye now."

Two bells rang and all at once the crewmen were coming on deck from the stern, from the bow, from below decks. They swarmed down the riggings. They came carrying rags and scrub brushes. One even had a squawking chicken under his arm. Under Mr. Forthinggale and the boatswain's eyes they fumbled themselves into two rows. I looked up and saw the lookout still in the crow's nest. There would be at least two seasoned pirates left in the wheelhouse, the navigator and another seaman. There would be men at the lines should the sails need attention. Cook must still be in the galley. The smell of cooking fish was in the air, making saliva spout into my mouth. The rest of them, I thought, were here.

I recognized Magruder and Bandit and Pork and Skelly and Gabby and Puce and I saw others, not yet known to me.

There was William. The setting sun was in his hair. He was bare to the waist, lean and smooth and golden. My breath caught. I thought about our kisses, how they would start and stop and start again. I though of how his lips were rough and hard and warm. I looked at him and remembered.

"Sebastian will be scrutinizin' all o' ye," the captain shouted. "Stand where ye be."

Someone called out. "We did this afore."

"Aye. And ye'll do it again when I tell ye to," Captain Moriarity said.

I limped to the line. Did I dare to stand close to William? Should I take a chance? I squeezed between him and the one-eyed man next to him but the man shouted, "Hey! What do ye think ye're doin'? Ye think 'cause I only got one eye I can't see what ye be's up to? Stand away, Mistress." His shout became louder. "Cap'n. I caught these two tryin' to be together. I'm tellin' ye, like ye ordered."

The captain's voice cut into me. "You! Get to the end of the line."

"Aye, Captain."

She grabbed my arm. "I'm not goin' to put up wi' any trouble from you. Stay away from him. Or ye'll be off at the first sight o' land."

I stood perfectly still. Turtle Island. Words jumped in my throat but I closed my mouth on them. I walked with my back straight and my head high to where she directed me. From that distance I watched.

Sebastian made his way along each line, stopping before every man, taking a turn around him in the way he had done with me, shaking his head. I did not see him nod once.

There were rumblings and grumblings and complaining, but no one moved.

The sun had set now and dark, like spilled ink, was spreading across the sea.

Sebastian had checked every man. Was it for signs of cholera? Or scurvy? Or perhaps some other disease?

I did not know. I did not take him for a doctor but perhaps, since he knew everything, he had some knowledge of medicine. I paid attention when he studied William and I was relieved when he shook his head. Whatever he was looking for, William was cleared.

"Finished, Captain," he said and she leaned down to him.

"Nothing?"

"Nothing," he said.

"Could I have been concerned for no reason?" she asked.

"I believe there is no need for ye to be anxious, Cap'n."

"But what is she after? Us?"

"I do not know. I do not even know that she is."

The captain seemed to be aware of me for the first time. "I was told ye disgorged yer last food," she said. "Eat now, then go to my cabin. Gummer will have the lamp lit. I saw ye pummel yer leg. Are they painin' ye?"

"Aye."

There is a jar of unguent on my table. Rub it on yer legs. 'Twill ease them."

I was amazed at this kindness. It was unexpected and I felt a rush of gratitude. "Thank ye, Captain," I said.

"There be's no need of thanks. I want ye ready to work wi' Sebastian in the mornin'. 'Tis not that I care for yer welfare."

"Aye, aye, Captain," I said.

There was a strong smell of cooking fish. There must have been a good catch. I knew the seas here were full of bonito and mullet, albacore and dolphin. It would likely be a fish stew.

It was a stew, thick and aromatic, plumping in a big cauldron. I straggled toward Cook with the others. Where was William? I couldn't see him in the snaggle of bodies around me. And then I did. He was pushing closer to where I stood, but not too close. He smiled at me and touched a finger to his lips and I surreptitiously touched mine in response.

At the wooden board where the stew was being ladled into bowls, he was two bodies away from me.

"I was caulking the hull up on the foredeck," he said loudly as if addressing the man next to him.

"Aye. We took a cannon shot there when we went after the *Corsair*," the man said, sticking his thumb in his stew and licking it. "Needs more salt, Cook," he called.

"Gi' it back if ye don't like it," Cook called back.

William had told me where he was and what he had been doing. I would get a message to him in the same way.

"Smells good," I said loudly, smiling at Cook's unresponsive face. "I was sewing on the sails with Sebastian. 'Twas hard work and I'm hungry."

I saw William pause.

Cook grunted. "Ye don't need to be tellin' me yer doin's, Mistress. I have no wish to hear. Move along."

I'm not telling you, you fool, I thought. I am speaking to my love as he spoke to me.

I seated myself on a crate and cradled my bowl of stew. When I leaned forward I could see William.

The stew reminded me of home. Carla, who cooked for my mother, took out the guts and chopped off the heads before she put the fish in the pot with the onions and potatoes. She never added spices. My mother liked plain food, the kind she'd had when she was a girl in Scotland. There were seasonings of some kind in this. Fish heads swam in the grease-filled broth, the eyes still in them, some eyes floating free. If the guts were out or not it did not seem to matter. On my spoon was a fish bladder, or perhaps an octopus tentacle. The spreading dark made it difficult to tell exactly but that did not matter either. I chewed greedily, and drank and drank from my mug of water. I would never get enough water.

Sebastian came toward me, balancing his bowl and a mug of brandy. I recognized the smell. It was the smell in our parlor that mixed with the smell of cigars when my father and his quartermaster drank together after my mother had retired for the night.

I made room beside me on the crate. "Do you wish to sit, Sebastian?"

He sat next to me, his short legs not reaching the deck.

There was a rough table, not big enough for the whole crew, and seated at it I saw Captain Moriarity.

"She does not eat privately, on her own?" I asked. Somehow, to see her there with the ordinary seamen, did not seem proper.

Sebastian smiled. "She is one of us. She eats with us." He took a drink, then shoveled stew into his mouth.

"It is good," I said.

"Aye and the drink." He took a swig and licked his lips. "Good French brandy, seized from the *Corsair*."

The man called Puce stopped next to us. "Sebastian?" he asked.

The bowl he held was empty and some of its contents were smeared on the front of his striped shirt. "Tell us what ye was lookin' for earlier? That was the first time on this journey. But she had us do that afore, two cruises ago. Does Cap'n seek to wed one o' us? Are you pickin' out the likeliest 'un."

Sebastian snorted. "If'n I was, I would never pick you."

He got a lewd gesture in response.

When Puce had wandered off I said, "What was the

reason for that inspection, Sebastian. Can you tell me?"

He drained his brandy. The green eyes met mine, those listening eyes.

"I will just say that the cap'n, God bless her, be's superstitious. She does not fear much. But she is afraid of evil spirits. That's all ye need to know. Ye should get to yer hammock now and don't forget to rub on that unguent afore ye sleep. I wants ye at the sails by sunrise."

I had been dismissed. I stood and my legs gave way beneath me. I stumbled and Sebastian caught me before I staggered. "Ye're wore out. But ye'll get used to the work."

I took a last look at William seated by the captain at the table. She must have summoned him beside her. She could be with him and I could not. If I wanted us both to live I would have to get used to that.

Chapter Eight

A hammock was already strung between two wall pegs. Who had done that? The one they called Gummer.

The captain would still be at the table, with William and the others. Had he noticed that I was gone? Did he hope to dream of me as I hoped to dream of him?

I found the bottle of unguent and read the label.

RELIEVES ACHES
ASSUAGES PAIN
STIMULATES HAIR GROWTH
EMULSIFIES SKIN

I sniffed it. The smell was powerful but not unpleasant. Before I applied it I needed to find the seats of easement. On the *Reprisal* they had been at the bow, under the red dragon figurehead. I had not seen them anywhere here.

I laid my flute on my hammock and went up on deck. It was true night now. A million stars speckled the sky and the *Sea Wolf* hissed softly through the sea as if she smelled the prey ahead and was following the scent.

I started toward the bow then saw a lone seaman leaning over the railing.

"Can you direct me to the seats of easement?" I asked him.

He stared at me blankly, then laughed, a roaring, raucous laugh. "By heaven, that be's a curious word for it. We just refers to it as the hole. Turn around. It be's back there at the stern, far as ye can go. But there be's no seats of easement girl. If ye want easement ye have to take yer chances."

"Thank you," I said with as much dignity as I could summon.

Another gust of laughter followed me as I went quickly to the stern.

"Don't fall in," he called.

There were indeed no seats. There was just a net with a hole in the middle that could swing out over the sea. It looked precarious but I climbed into it and pushed away from the deck. Underneath me was moving black water with a topping of white foam. I was thrown this way and that in the net cradle as it creaked and scraped against the hull. Up and down, side to side at the mercy of the ship. It was a strange contraption but it sufficed. When I was ready I pulled myself back to safety using the wooden bar at the side.

The captain was not yet back in the cabin. She might have been attending to her duties or still sitting at the table with William. I told myself it did not concern me, but it did.

I took off my green pantaloons and rubbed my legs that were sore to the touch. I kneaded my fingertips. The bleeding on them had stopped but when I examined them under the lamp I saw small pink puncture wounds.

In the bundle of clothes we'd taken from the sea chest I found a red-striped jersey, stained and torn at one armpit but better than the one I wore, the one Jenks had given me when I first fell onto the deck of the *Sea Wolf*. Could it have been only this morning? Could it have been only last night that William and I were together, facing death on Pox Island? Do not think of this now, Catherine, I told myself. Do not.

Bent over I could step inside the cupboard to change

my shirt. The door to the cabin was open and I had no trust of the pirates on the *Sea Wolf* although the captain had given them such strong warnings to keep away from me. I changed my shirt, then took my flute and sat in the throne chair.

Softly I played, ignoring the stinging of my fingertips.

"Come home from the sea, my darlin', my dear,
Come home from the sea to me."

My mother loved this plaintive, sorrowful song. She told me it was about a fisherman's wife waiting for him on the rocks while his fishing boat was caught in a storm. My mother's eyes would well with tears and I always knew that when she listened to it she was thinking not of that fisherman but of my father, off somewhere on the high seas in the *Reprisal*. Come home to me, my darling, my dear. My husband.

Foolish of me tonight to play a song so slow and sorrowful. I changed to another for myself. "Dancin' a jig at Mahoney's Pub." It wanted to be loud and merry but I played it softly. No need to attract attention.

I eyed the books on the shelf, then got up and pulled out *The Tain*.

Medb, Queen of Connacht, proud, imperious, strong,

confident. I turned page after page, fascinated by her likeness to Captain Medb Moriarity.

She came into the cabin.

Immediately I was uneasy.

"You are reading?" she asked.

"Aye." I jumped up to replace the book on the shelf, wishing I had not taken such a liberty with her possessions.

"Sit ye down then and read aloud. It is a long time since my father read to me from *The Tain*. Read to me of Medb and the bull. He named me after her. He told me I would grow to be a woman like her, strong and fearless."

I sat again in the chair, thankful that there was to be no recrimination. She closed the cabin door.

I kept my head bent over the book as I sensed her remove whatever garments she removed at night. I heard the lid being lifted off the commode and the unmistakable sounds of the captain relieving herself. Sebastian had said she was "one of us." But it was apparent she did her most intimate toiletries here in her cabin. Not for her the rope swing with the well-placed hole.

She rummaged around on the long table and held up a key.

"I do not lock my door. There is not a man in my crew that would dare to come in here while I sleep. But ye might decide to go out and see if ye can find him. Ye knows who I mean. I will not have that."

She turned the key then placed it under the roll of clothing she had at the head of her bed.

There was a creaking as she lay down. "Read girl! Read!" she ordered.

I began at the beginning. "How Conchobor was begotten," I read.

"Ye can leave that out. Get to the part about Queen Medb and the bull."

I leafed through the pages.

"She wanted the bull," the captain said. "They wouldn't sell it to her so she went to war to get it."

"Aye," I said, wondering if I should pay her full attention or continue to look for the chapters on the great warrior queen.

She fought for what she wanted, as I do. She fought and killed as I have done." There was a silence. I did not move, awaiting her pleasure. She waved her hand. "I am too tired to listen tonight. Tomorrow night ye will continue. You will read to me when I summon ye. While ye be's here," she added. "It pleases me."

"Aye, Captain." I closed the book and put it back in its slot.

I would read. While I was here.

She shuttered the lantern.

A half moon peered in through the porthole.

I climbed into the hammock, feeling the sway of the ship under me. I was wearied but my mind was active. I heard the lantern swing with the movement, saw its dull shine. I could smell the unguent on my legs but it had not eased their aching.

In her bed Captain Moriarity snored, little puffy snores.

I was close to sleep when I heard the smallest of sounds.

I sat up, almost tipping myself onto the floor, peering through the darkness. Moonlight touched the handle of the cabin door. It was turned gently, turned again.

Someone, not aware of the lock, was trying to get in.

I watched, fascinated, thoughts tumbling around in my head.

Was it an emergency, one of the crew needing to get to the captain?

No, because there was no calling of her name, no heavy knock.

Or could it be William? My heart leaped. William!

I swung out of the hammock and tiptoed to the door through the path of moonlight. "William?"

From the captain's bed came the undisturbed snores, as even as breathing.

"William?" I whispered again.

But there was no answer. The doorknob was still.

I stood, staring at the painted wood of it. There was a drawing of a cross in the center, a cross with a faded green circle round the top. A Celtic cross. I had seen drawings of it before. Protection, I thought. Or superstition?

All was quiet. Whoever had been outside was gone.

Chapter Nine

I was up early with Sebastian, sewing on the sails, ready for the sunrise that didn't come. The sea and sky were covered with a gray fog that lay across the deck like a winding sheet. It was in my hair. It chilled my bones and I realized that my aches ached worse with the cold and wetness of it.

Around me the crew was already at work. The guns were polished and checked, the boards scrubbed, the railings rubbed.

"We keeps the *Sea Wolf* rubbed up even in fog," Sebastian said.

"Seems like time wasted," I said.

"We has our duties. If'n we slack, the cap'n'll be on us. There'll be punishment, ye can lay to that."

I stole a glance at him. Skelly had told me that Sebastian liked to talk. I chanced a remark.

"I find it strange that a woman captain can control a crew as she does."

"May be." Sebastian pulled himself another strand of hemp and threaded his needle. "They respect her and fear her. Ye have not had time to see her in battle. She is a wild beast. Or when she is angry. I seen her chop off a finger when it went a place it should not have gone in her presence." He paused. "There's not another captain can smell out a treasure like she does. There's greed in the crew. It's worth being ruled by a woman if'n the rewards are good. They be's grateful for that, and more."

The sail I was stitching was fog damp and the needle slippery. I struggled with it. Sebastian leaned across me and gave it a last push through the wet canvas. He went on.

"Aye, they gots a lot to be grateful for. No other cap'n would have a one o' them. They be's half blind, half crippled, one handless, one footless. One can't talk, one can't hear and Gummer, he be's older than the ocean. And who but Captain Moriarity would a' taken me, me, a dwarf?" He gave a small chuckle. "I tole her a dwarf was lucky on a ship. Good news for me that she be's superstitious. I tole her I had the Light of Foresight and she believed me. 'Twas true. I have. We be's all loyal to her. There's not a man would fail her."

I peered in front of me.

A sailor was leaning overboard, lowering a leaded weight through the fog and into the water, calling out "three fathoms," then "four fathoms," then three again.

"We be's extra careful when the fog lies on the sea," Sebastian said. "There be's hidden dangers hereabouts. Ye can run up on shoals or break yer hull on a sunk wreck. Like the *Isabella*."

"She broke her hull?"

"Aye, but she made it to shore. Cap'n has informers. We know where she be's lyin' and what's aboard her."

"The informers will be rewarded?" I asked tartly.

"Oh aye. Ye can be sure o' that."

We sewed for a while without talking.

By noontime the fog lifted and the sun appeared.

I found myself secretly examining every pirate that passed us by. Who was it who'd tried to get in the captain's cabin last night? Had it been that one with the limping leg? Or this one, with the pustules, red and oozing on his cheeks? Should I tell Sebastian? No, he'd likely report to the captain and who knew what she might do.

Now and then I'd stretch my legs to ease them. Once Sebastian said, "Stand up, Mistress. Take a step or two. There's no need for ye to cripple yerself."

I stood gratefully.

Mr. Forthinggale came upon me as I stood, bending my back, stamping my feet to flow blood into them. "Get back to work," he said. "You're not on board for yer pleasure." Before I could answer Sebastian said, "I tole her to stand, Quarter. She be's no good to me if she's squirmin' around like an eel on a hot rock."

The quartermaster humphed, then strode away.

William, where are you? If only I could talk to you, tell you my fears, ask you. Ask you what the captain says to you when I am not there.

I saw no sign of him, not all the morning long nor when we stopped for maggoty hardtack and dried beef in the middle of the day. There were limes and we each took one.

"Suck on it," Sebastian said. " 'Twill keep away the scurvy. 'Tis a new and remarkable discovery. Have ye seen scurvy, girl? If'n ye did ye'd chew that lime, skin an' all. 'Tis worth a bit o' sourness in yer mouth."

I took a bite and felt my eyes water and my throat curl up. Sebastian began to tell me about scurvy, how it makes your gums go black and your teeth fall out. How it rashes you all over your body and how you go out of your mind at the end and see mermaids in the rigging and Davy Jones inviting you down to the depths to sup with him.

I could not keep my mind steady, nor my heart that longed for William.

Sebastian stopped talking and looked closely at me with those green knowing eyes. "He be's in the wheel-house with the cap'n; Finnegan says she's learnin' him how to measure the distance sailed from day to day and how to chart the ship's position."

I nodded. My throat stung and I didn't know if it was with tears or with the bitter juice of the lime. Captains did not teach ordinary seamen, or cabin boys, unless it was for a reason. Unless they had future hopes for them. Unless they were keeping them.

The ship moved sluggishly, the sails empty.

"The fog eats the wind," Sebastian said. "No wind, no speed."

We sewed all day. My fingers were raw. I sucked them and did not complain.

The rip I was working on was almost closed.

"Am I useful to you?" I asked Sebastian.

"Aye," he said. "You be's as useful as Blunt was. He was a grand worker afore a shell from the Barbary Blue blew out his belly. He lay on the deck here wi' his guts squeezin' through his fingers. 'Twas good for me that I got a replacement." He looked slyly at me, then said, "Aye ye're useful. I'll be tellin' the cap'n."

I did not see William. He was not at the table when we went for food at sunset. I did not see the captain either.

There was soup with potatoes in it and a scrap or two of yesterday's fish. There was ale and water.

I ate little.

⚓

There was no reading to the captain that night. When she came in the cabin she took the key from the pocket of her trousers and locked the door. I feigned sleep as she took care of her needs, laid her hand on the Celtic cross, got into bed. She was humming a tune that was unknown to me. I wondered what she was thinking and of whom, and what it was that had put her in such high spirits. I thought I knew, but the thought hurt too much and I let go of it. At least she wasn't with him now and I could be thankful for that. Soon her humming changed to her small fat snores and I knew she slept.

I ached all over. The unguent did not help.

But I, too, slept at last. And if someone tried to get into our locked cabin I did not hear it.

⚓

Morning came. I worked all that day and the day after that. Nights I read aloud from *The Tain*.

On the third day we passed at a distance from a bare rock that rose out of the sea like a monstrous sleeping whale.

"Turtle Island," Sebastian said. "You'll not be marooned on that one, Cate." He had come to calling me Cate in a friendly way which made our work together more tolerable.

I gazed at Turtle Island, my heart beating too fast. Would I ever again hear the word island without this breath-stopping panic?

William passed by one time, rolling a barrel of water. I thought quickly. "I never see my friend William," I said to Sebastian in my most carrying voice. "I miss him every day."

William paused. "Sebastian," he said. "I think o' my friend every minute. But it must be endured."

"Are ye speakin' to me?" Sebastian asked. "Better get on wi' yer work."

"Aye," William said.

I watched him till he was out of sight.

"'Twill not be good to be smarter that Captain Moriarity," Sebastian said. "She has no likin' for disobedience."

"What disobedience do you speak of?" I asked and he fixed me with his green stare, shrugged and went back to his stitching.

I got to recognize some of the crew as they stopped to exchange words with Sebastian. Horn, who spoke with such difficulty that he mostly signed with his small, calloused hands. Catman who was friend to the ship's black cat, the wild creature that would not let anyone else touch her. Claw, so called for the metal apparatus he had in place of a hand. I kept a watch out for the man with the missing finger that the captain had cut off when he used it inappropriately in her presence but did not see him. Magruder, leering and squinting, made every excuse to stop and stare greedily at me.

"I might mention to the cap'n that you doesn't have enough work to do," Sebastian told him once and Magruder said, "Aye, ye better do that, ye mealy little midget."

"Go," Sebastian said. "And next time ye come this way, do not stop."

Then, one night when Sebastian's weather string had warned him of a savage storm fast approaching, William and I met by chance, alone on the rolling deck. The *Sea*

Wolf pitched and yawed. The sea around was fierce, frosted with white foam that spat at the ship. Wind tore at the reefed sails, trying to loose them. The crew was busy, battening hatches, tying down anything the storm might take. Rain drummed on the deck.

First he was only a shadow, coming toward me.

Then he was William.

We clung to each other. There was little time for words. Someone could come at any minute. There was just the warmth of our kisses that mixed with the rain beating on us. "Me love. My darlin' girl," he whispered. On the island, when we came out of the sea, we'd been wet like this. Those kisses and those holdings had been the sweetest.

I ran my hand through his hair, felt under my fingers the thin line of scar on his face, stood tiptoe to kiss it.

"I don't think I can bear it."

My words were muffled against his chest.

"Shh, shh. We have to keep on livin'. We have to do anything, say anything to hang on. The voyage will end."

A sob rose in my throat. "What if she decides I am to be marooned again, alone? She will never let you go."

"If she tried to keep me 'twould be in vain. I'd jump after ye. Beelzebub himself could not stop me."

There was an urgent whisper behind us that was almost lost in the wind.

Skelly!

"Get yerselves away! Puce and Skull be's comin'. Hurry!"

There was no time for a goodbye word. We moved quickly in opposite directions.

Back along the deck, fighting the force of the gale I saw Sebastian.

He stood with his arms wide, his back to the wind. In one hand he held his knotted string. "Aye," he said. "I told cap'n 'twould be a storm to remember. 'Tis true. But 'twill not be a hurricane. There is no eye. Me and my string can always tell."

It was a savage storm, two days long.

When it was over the ship had a battered look to her and the crew started again, scrubbing and cleaning and polishing. The bilges were full of water and needed pumping. Sails were spread to dry.

Sebastian and I worked on wet canvas, so heavy that it numbed my legs. "Me own short legs be's an advantage," he said. "They bend on themselves easier."

Nights I read to the captain. I thought perhaps the night reading would make her softer to me but that did not happen. It was when she chose *Gulliver's Travels* that it became apparent to me that she did not know how to read. She had tired of *The Tain* and said, "Pick another book, Catherine, and continue."

"Which one, Captain?" I asked. "The one there, with the green cover," she said impatiently. The title, *Gulliver's Travels*, was writ plain across the front.

"Aye, that 'un," she'd said. "What is it called?"

I told her and explained what it was about.

"'Twill do." She said nothing more. Captain Moriarity was not one to expose a frailty. But I knew. I tucked the knowledge away in my mind. It might be useful.

Every night we had the same routine. We slept in the clothes we had worn that day. She used the commode, I went to the cradle at the back, hanging out above the ocean as the ship bucked beneath me like a horse I had one time ridden. Sometimes she washed her face and hands with water. Sometimes she did not. I could use a bucket of water that Gummer placed outside the door to wash myself.

Every night she ran her hand over the painted cross on the door and muttered words that I could not hear. Every night she touched the lid of the box that I knew held William's hair and once I saw her take out the lock of his hair and press it to her lips. She shuttered the lamp. She did not wish me goodnight and I did not bid her a good night either. Soon I heard her snores, like high-pitched whistles, like the sound of a repetitive high note on my flute. She never mentioned my music nor invited me to play it. I could not anyway, not even for myself now. The tips of my fingers were so raw and painful that they bled at the slightest touch.

Each morning I took my place with Sebastian on the deck. One day we met up with a small merchant vessel sailing in the opposite direction. I looked at it and wished with all my heart that William and I were on board it, heading for Port Teresa.

"Cap'n won't be stoppin' to plunder that 'un," Sebastian said. "Even though it be's a young chicken waitin' to be plucked, Cap'n be's after bigger prizes."

First the *Reprisal*, I knew. Then the *Isabella*.

Every morning the wild black cat slunk past us carrying a dead and bloody rat in its teeth. "It be's lookin' for Catman," Sebastian said with a chuckle. "It likes to be givin' him presents. There be's plenty more where that one came from."

Around us the men worked, repairing, splicing ropes, checking the cannons, polishing and sharpening their knives and their cutlasses for the battles to come.

" 'Tis good they have plenty to do," Sebastian said. "They gets bored if'n there's no fightin' and no booty and little to occupy them. They needs to have a bit o' fightin' to spur their spirits and a goodly plunder to keep 'em happy."

It was the very next day that the lookout spotted a sailing ship and called it out.

The *Reprisal!*

I recognized it from a distance and I was overcome by a mixture of sorrow and vindictiveness at the sight of it. My father's ship that he had loved. My father's ship with Herc as captain.

Captain Moriarity strode along the deck and stopped where we sat.

"A word with ye, Sebastian," she said.

Sebastian slid out from under the sail and stood, flexing his legs, stretching his arms. The two of them moved away but I heard the captain ask, "What are the portents, Sebastian? Have ye consulted them?"

"They are good, Cap'n," Sebastian said. "We are in unison with the sun and stars. 'Tis Monday, a good day for a battle. I see a conundrum, and an unanswered question. But in the end 'twill go your way."

"So be it," she said. "I am accustomed to getting my way."

She shouted an order and the false English flag was run down the masthead. Quickly, quickly, as if it had been waiting for the opportunity, the Skull and Crossbones swooped to the mast top and screamed its business to the wind.

I took a deep breath. Whatever was to happen next would happen.

Chapter Ten

The men of the *Sea Wolf* yelled and threw around curses, which was their way of rejoicing. They tossed anything that was at hand, including each other, into the air. I thought, as I had thought before, that they were like children, kept inside and then let loose. But they were dangerous children.

Captain Moriarity addressed them. " 'Twill not be as good a booty as we'll get from the *Isabella*," she said. "But we'll stop this belly-suckin' excuse for a ship now. She could not get there afore us. Our speed surpasses hers. But she could come after us, lookin' for a share. We're two days, maybe three, from our big prize and we wants no extra trouble when we gets there. Think o' this as sport and a warmin' up for what's ahead. Are yez all wi' me?"

"Aye, Cap'n. Aye."

"There'll be something on this belly-suckin' ship worth takin'."

"We likes a challenge."

There was a frenzy in their response.

"To yer places then," the captain said.

The *Sea Wolf* came up behind the *Reprisal*.

"She's tryin' to run," Captain Moriarity said, looking through her spyglass. "But we'll give her no quarter."

The arms chest was unlocked and the men took weapons, muskets, flintlock pistols, and small pomegranate-shaped objects made of wood that I did not recognize.

I did not avail myself of those but chose a pistol.

Puce grinned, weighing one of the pomegranates in his hand. "Grenado shells. They's full o' gunpowder. Light these wicks, lob a few o' them into the ship and it blasts them to Davy Jones right quick."

I shuddered. What devil's devices were these? I had never seen them on the *Reprisal*.

The men swarmed to the starboard railings. Excitement, expectation, and greed spread like a flame as the ships drew closer. There was a babble of anticipation.

" 'Twill be an easy catch," someone shouted. "We gots 'em outnumbered and outgunned."

"By Billy's bodkin there'll be hogsheads o' rum the night," another called.

I looked for William and saw him. Our eyes met and unspoken words passed between us. He stepped away from the others and I moved beside him. The crew, intent on the prey, had their backs to us. Gabby did turn, saw us and turned back immediately to watch the *Reprisal*. He had other overwhelming interests.

William and I stood, face to face.

He ran a finger along my lips and I closed my eyes. It wasn't even a kiss. But it filled me. Would I ever get enough of his touch, of the way my bones seemed to dissolve when I was close to him?

His lips brushed my ear. "I remember," he whispered, and then he was gone, joining the rest of the men by the railing.

The captain stood alongside the quartermaster and the boatswain.

She was yelling at the shadow crew on the *Reprisal*.

"Ahoy!" she called. "Aboard the *Reprisal*. I am captain on the ship, *Sea Wolf*. We aim to take yer vessel. Do ye surrender or will we blow ye out o' the water?"

The answer was not long in coming.

There was a fusillade of small arms fire from the *Reprisal* and then a thunderous cannon blast. It was aimed too high and smashed harmlessly in the sea behind us.

I imagined the deck of the *Reprisal*, the pirates I had known scrambling about, loading the cannons, preparing to be boarded. Fish and fat Red... and Cook who had thrown us a small bundle of food when we were to be marooned. And there would be Herc and Hopper.

The cannons of the *Sea Wolf* were ready, the powder kegs beside them, awaiting the gun master's order to fire.

"Fire!"

Boom, boom, boom.

One blast hit the *Reprisal*'s main mast. One of her topsail spars hung, cracked and crooked.

Another blast smashed into the hull tearing open a hole.

From the *Reprisal* came two cannon shots in retaliation. One hit our big, square foresail. I looked up and saw the way it hung in tatters and thought vaguely that it would need a lot of stitching to make it seaworthy again. The second shot sizzled harmlessly across the bow.

Now the two ships were close, so close that I could see a figure I knew to be Herc on the deck and beside him a one-legged man, balancing on a crutch. Herc and Hopper.

Small-arms fire from both sides spattered the hulls of the two ships.

Then I heard Captain Moriarity's voice. "Where's Ronan? Get him up here. Give him the grenades."

Beside me Puce said to the pock-faced pirate next to him, "Oh aye, bring us Ronan. He can hit a bird in the eye wi' one o' them grenades."

They made way for a tall, gangly pirate I'd seen many times before. I'd thought him feebleminded, the way his head bobbed and his legs and arms splayed out as if he didn't know what to do with them. But he knew what to do with the grenades.

One after the other he threw them unerringly onto the *Reprisal*'s deck.

One after the other came the violent detonations, followed by screams and obscenities that shattered the space between us. Followed by the cheers and cavorting of the *Sea Wolf*'s crew.

"Is it necessary to kill them all?" I asked Captain Moriarity, the words coming before I could stop them.

"Are ye a driveling nincompoop?" she asked, her cold stare fixing me like a fish on a hook.

"The more we kill, the more for us," someone shouted cheerfully but another voice said, "Shut the wench up, Cap'n. We gots no need of stupid words afore we do battle."

I bit my lip and said no more.

Now the *Reprisal* was wallowing drunkenly in the water, listing heavily to port.

"Ye can stop now, Ronan. Ye did well," Captain Moriarity shouted. "Do ye surrender?" she called to the *Reprisal*.

"Never," came the answer accompanied by a string of vile obscenities and a straggle of pistol shots. Herc's voice. I would know it anywhere. I thought I could smell him even through the reek of gunpowder.

Again our cannons boomed.

"Do ye surrender?" Captain Moriarity called.

This time the answer came. "Devil take ye for a passel of mangy curs. We'll fight till the end. Come and see if ye can lay hold on us. We'll be ready for ye."

There was a cheer from the *Sea Wolf* crew. It was evident that there was nothing they liked more than close conflict.

The men threw grappling hooks and pushed and shoved to be among the first to board the *Reprisal*. Shots spurted around them as they clambered across the rope. I saw blood on Puce's shoulder but he kept going along, hand over hand, not knowing or not caring that he had been hit. I saw the captain, swarming ahead of the others, shouting threats as she went.

I tucked my pistol in the band of my green pantaloons

along with the knife and my flute. There would be no need of my flute but I was never comfortable if I was parted from it.

Ahead of me, Sebastian grasped the rope with his arms and legs like some kind of a great ape.

I saw William.

How strange it was that he and I were going back on the *Reprisal* and in such a way. We had left it in a long-boat, doomed never to see it or those in it or another living being ever again. He saw me and shouted, "Stay away from Herc. If'n he sees ye he'll kill ye."

I did not need to be told.

"You, too," I shouted.

The crossing was formidable though short. The two ships rolled in the water, one tilting up on a surge, one tilting down as if playing some sort of child's game. The rope was slippery and rough to hold on to and the men in front and behind jerked on it with every movement. One man fell off with a splash into the trough of a wave below. I thought it was Pork.

None stopped to look how he was faring. Perhaps he could swim but it was unlikely.

Behind me someone shoved and yelled, "What are ye waitin' for? Keep moving, wench, or I'll knock ye down to the sharks."

I got to the end of the rope and pulled myself over the side, onto the *Reprisal*'s deck.

There was such a hubbub, such noise and screams. Hand to hand, cutlasses flashing, the fighting had started.

On the port side of the ship, water sloshed through the hole in the hull, running in dirty streams along the slant of the deck. The crosswise timber suspending the mainsail hung at an angle and the canvas sagged, pulled down by its own weight.

"Careful above," I shouted. "The sail's going to fall."

Nobody looked or answered.

I moved away should it crash below.

I had left my shoes behind on the *Reprisal* the better to have a purchase on the rope and now I stood barefoot in frigid seawater that was slurped pink with blood. My foot touched something red and slimy. Sickness rose in my throat but I held it down, reminding myself that I was a pirate captain's daughter and a pirate myself now. And this was what pirates did.

The crew of the *Sea Wolf* went wild. They tore open the hatches, cut apart bales and trunks with their cutlasses. What they had no use for they hacked to pieces and tossed overboard. They swore and invoked the devil and called upon different saints and laughed like maniacs.

Captain Moriarity was among them making no

attempt to quell them, joining in the mayhem.

And all the time the *Reprisal* canted lower in the greedy sea that sucked at her deck and carried with it anything that floated free.

I recognized many of my father's old crew, those who had mocked me and spat on me and pushed me off to a certain death on Pox Island. But now I had only pity for them. They were huddled in groups like whipped dogs, making halfhearted attempts to protect the ship and themselves.

One of the *Sea Wolf*'s men shouted, "There be's barrels o' gunpowder below. Come on," and I saw William, following some of the others, helping to heave the barrels of gunpowder to the side to be transferred to our ship.

"Are ye all right?" he shouted to me.

"Aye. And you?"

He nodded.

I had a moment's confusion. They were transferring from my father's ship, the ship I had dreamed of all my life, to this other ship that was now "ours." But with Herc as captain, the *Reprisal* was no longer mine. With Captain Moriarity, I did not know.

Sebastian lurched along the deck, slicing at legs with his boarding axe. When he saw me he shouted, "I be's good at this. They never looks down until I've about chopped their legs out from under them."

At that minute I got my first glimpse of Red, my old friend from the *Reprisal*. His fat belly was bare, the ginger hairs on his chest matted with blood. He was fighting and swearing. "Ye maggots! Ye plague-infested bilge rats." I had no time to hail him for I was being attacked from the side by Mr. Trimble, quartermaster on the *Reprisal*. He raised his cutlass above my head but when he did I spoke his name. He stared in disbelief then lowered the weapon. "You!" he said. "How can it be you?"

I did not answer and he stood, stupefied and still staring.

And then I saw Herc. I had forgotten he was so massive a creature, obese and greasy. Hercules, shortened to Herc. He stood motionless in a corner by the bow, his back protected by the bulwark behind him. When he saw me, he took a step forward and stared in disbelief. His shirt was torn, the rag around his head soaked with blood. "Are ye a ghost, ye sorry wench?" he stammered.

"Aye, I am the ghost of Pox Island, come back to take my revenge," I said. It was a glorious moment to see how his face paled. I jumped forward and grabbed his hair that stuck out above the head rag, putting my knife to his throat, forcing him down on the deck. The putrid smell of him, the stench of blood and sweat sickened my nose.

All around us was chaos.

Sebastian had come, panting, beside me. "This is the hog-faced bottom feeder what put ye off?" he asked. No need for Sebastian to lean over to stick his face next to Herc's. One half-lying, the other standing they were on the same level.

"Finish him, Cate, or I'll do it for ye."

"Hold off!" Herc shouted. "I am captain of this ship and I demand to speak wi' yer cap'n. 'Tis me right!"

A small bunch of the *Sea Wolf*'s crew, wheezing and gasping for breath, had moved to mass around us and there was Captain Moriarity, her eyes red as coals.

"I am captain of the *Sea Wolf*. Put up yer knife, Cate."

"Cate is it!" Herc said in a disgusted voice. "Let me up, ye besom!"

He rose shakily and straightened his shirt. "From the sound o' yer voice I knowed ye to be a woman!" he said, glaring at Captain Moriarity. "A woman's got no place."

"Hush yer mouth," Captain Moriarity growled.

"I know who ye are! I heard o' ye. Ye be's the one they calls the She-Wolf o' the Caribbean."

"Aye," Captain Moriarity grinned her she-wolf grin. Her nose wrinkled. "What is that foul odor? 'Tis not a fightin' stink."

"It is him," I said. "Herc. Ye could smell him from ship's bow to stern."

Herc pointed his thumb at me. "This wench is nothin' but trouble. Her and the scurrilous puppy she took up wi' on me ship."

"Your ship?" I could not stay quiet. "My father's ship. Never yours, though you took it over as captain when he died."

I sensed Captain Moriarity beside me, felt the heat of her, heard her labored breath. Blood ran from a gash on her arm over her hand, the hand that held a cutlass.

"What did the wench and the scurrilous puppy do to ye?" she asked. Her voice was dangerously quiet.

"She lied and deceived, sayin' she was a boy and the rotten puppy aided her. When I gave him the just punishment of the cat she thwarted it. She stopped the lashin' afore it had right started."

He spat at my feet, the spittle floating off in the blood and water that coursed along the deck. I fixed him with a hatred-filled stare remembering for an instant the day of William's lashing, the long, braided tails of the cat o' nine tails cutting down on his back, Mr. Trimble's arm rising and falling as he leveled the punishment. It had been raining, I remembered.

I swallowed to ease the burn in my throat. How I had

longed to help William. How I had loved him.

Herc was still talking.

"Ye knows, Cap'n, that orders must be obeyed. She defied me. I made the right decision to get the both o' them off of me ship and that order was carried out. By me kind grace they were given food and water to keep them livin' for a few days."

"Aye. I can surmise how much food and water ye gave them." The captain wiped her cutlass on her trousers and examined the blade. "I have no disagreement wi' ye orderin' punishments," she said. "My crew must obey me at all times. Me authority is absolute. But I will tell ye, 'tis yer bad luck that I've taken a likin' to the young 'un."

Not to me, I thought. There is no liking for me.

"Oh aye," Herc leered. "I hear tell old women likes 'em young. I hear tell it makes them feel young again theirselves."

"Shut yer mouth," William yelled. I hadn't seen him come up to stand at the back of the others. But his words did not come in time to stop those of the crew who had heard Herc from tittering and nudging one another. I saw them exchange winks and grins.

Herc scowled and pointed at William. "Ye be's a worthless dog."

He leered at Captain Moriarty. "The boy's a worthless

dog, I tell ye, and not worth your notice. Ye need a man around, not a whelp like this 'un."

How foolish of him, I thought. She is the vanquisher, he is the vanquished. Why does he not know to be quiet?

Captain Moriarity moved so fast that I had time only to see the flash of the cutlass, hear Herc's short squeak before he fell to his knees and toppled over. I heard the gurgle of his breath leaving him.

We all stood there, silent, looking down at his lifeless body.

Chapter Eleven

"I meant only to teach him some respect," Captain Moriarity said.

" 'Tis too bad, but perhaps no great loss."

"Shall we throw him over or leave him be?" someone asked.

"He will be left for the crew of his own ship. Beg pardon, Cate. Of yer father's ship."

I tried to hide the shock I felt, not only because of Herc's sudden death, but because of Captain Moriarity's ruthless action. He had insulted the captain and he had spoken ill of William. And he had paid a terrible price.

I would not wish this death upon my worst enemy,

I thought, and he was my worst enemy. He was the one who happily planned a slow, painful end for William and me. But he was gone now and if I could not forgive I could show some deference for the dead. And what of his terrible, odious brother Hopper, who had been as villainous as he?

"He has a brother on the ship," I said. "He's..." I glanced up at the familiar frightening sound of Hopper's wooden leg tapping toward us.

The tapping stopped.

Hopper looked down at Herc then knelt beside him, his crutch sticking out behind him. He gently pushed the hair that was thick with blood away from his brother's face. Whatever words he whispered were not discernible even through the silence of the pirates gathered around us.

Perhaps there is love in him, I thought. Until now he has kept it well hidden.

He looked up. "Which of yez did this?" he asked.

"I did," Captain Moriarity's voice was strong and untroubled. "I listened to him with the courtesy of one captain for another. But I found him offensive and without respect for me or my crew. I exercised the just right of the victor."

Hopper crawled himself up. "Aye, 'twas was yer right,"

he said. " 'Tis my sorrow. I will care for him. No one else must touch him."

I had never imagined I would see Hopper dignified. But at this moment he was.

It was William who stepped forward and asked, "Ye need help to lift him, Hopper?" and it was Hopper who become his true self and spat at William. "Not from you, ye turncoat. This was your ship."

"Aye." William gave a short laugh. "I'm a turncoat who was sentenced to death by you and your brother. I owe ye no loyalty."

The heat was out of the fighting. There were just the sounds of scattered shots and men's voices raised in anger or mockery.

Mr. Trimble stepped forward—Mr. Trimble, false friend to my father and my mother. I could hardly find it in my heart to look at him. He had had the chance to speak up and save William and me when we had been in mortal danger and he had kept silent.

"Captain Moriarity," he said. "There is disarray amongst the crew of our ship. We have no captain at this time. There are two men in need of burying. We ask leave to surrender and will be grateful if you will spare our vessel."

"Done," Captain Moriarity said breezily. It was as if

Herc's death had never happened though the body lay at our feet.

How could she so easily dismiss it? Because she was arrogant and merciless and a pirate captain, I thought. I had known before that she had these attributes. But now I had seen them for myself.

I glanced at William. She would be merciless with us. She had told me once that her namesake, Medb, Queen of Connacht, fought for what she wanted. "As I do," she'd said.

I had no doubt that this Queen of the *Sea Wolf* wanted William.

⚓

Captain Moriarity ordered what plunder there was aboard the *Reprisal* to be collected and made ready to be transferred to the *Sea Wolf*.

"We got the gunpowder already," the boatswain, whose name I didn't know, told her.

"Well get whatever's of use to us and you men take whatever you fancy. Ye fought well."

There were barrels of grain and flour and salt set in a pile for the longboats. There were casks of wine and a few hens. There was salt pork and dried beef.

"Leave 'em something," the captain said. "We have no need for them to starve."

She addressed Mr. Trimble. "I will not burn yer ship nor sink her, Quartermaster. Ye can limp to the closest island and make repairs. I have spent enough time here and done what I needed to do."

I saw Red again. His ear was slashed and hanging loose from his head. His hand was capped around it but he still managed to grin at me.

"Ye're alive. Ye fooled them all. Ye always was a bold one."

"Ye fat little toad." Hopper lifted his crutch to strike him but I knocked it from his hand.

"Do yez have a doctor?" Captain Moriarity asked.

"No, Captain," Mr. Trimble answered, tightlipped. I was aware of how he never looked at me. "But we have our carpenter who is skilled in surgery and can set bones and sew."

"And cut," yelled one of the crew that I recognized. "He be's great wi' the saw."

It had been the carpenter who'd sawn off Hopper's leg, I remembered.

"I was not regardful of yer injuries," Captain Moriarity said coldly. "If ye had a doctor I planned on taking him with us. I will leave yer carpenter. Ye'll have need of him for yer repairs. Does any other man among ye want to join my crew and sail wi' us on the *Sea Wolf*?"

"Aye," a voice called and one pirate stepped forward. He was Clegg. I knew him from the time I thought he had drowned when the *Reprisal* was attacking the *Golden Bird*.

"What have ye to recommend ye?" Captain Moriarity asked.

"I am a gunner and good wi' all kind of explosives," Clegg said. "I have had no experience with the grenades ye threw but I am good wi' the cannons and wi' small arms."

The captain nodded. "We'll take ye wi' us."

Another shuffled forward. "Flanagan," he said. "I am of Ireland, like yerself, Cap'n."

"That's good enough for me," she answered.

"Red?" William called out. "Would you want to come?" To the captain he said, "Red was friend to the two o' us."

I waited for the captain to rebuke William for interfering but she only asked, "Which one o' ye be's Red?"

I should know by now that she is not going to rebuke William for anything, I thought. Except for loving me.

Red stepped forward. "They call me Red," he said.

"You want to sail wi' us?"

Red shook his head and drops of blood from his ear spattered the deck. "I will stay wi' the ship I came on," he said. "Ye'll pardon me mawkish sentiments, Cap'n. But I have sailed on the *Reprisal* for the past sixteen years. I have only two things in me life. Me fiddle and this ship. I will keep the both o' them." He paused and looked at me. "Unless ye needs me with ye, girl?"

"No," I said. "I have William." I did not glance at all at the captain.

"I be watchin' out for her, ye can lay to that, Red," William said and he smiled at me, that dazzle of a smile that made my heart leap.

"Enough." Captain Moriarity's voice expressed her annoyance.

She nodded toward Red. "Get yer carpenter to sew up that ear. And good luck to ye. The rest of yez, finish off. Take whatever we can use."

I took one last look at Herc, lying on the deck, Hopper standing over him like a sentry on guard. The injured ship pitched under my feet as I slipped away.

Chapter Twelve

I thought Daisy and Pansy knew me as I came to their pen. I spoke softly to them. "Did you miss me? I miss you." I bent across the enclosure and kissed the wiry, goat-smelling top of Daisy's head. "I thought perhaps to take you with me on the *Sea Wolf*. But your fate would be the same there as here. And I hope that perchance when this ship is careened for repairs you will be free, for a while. You might get to roam under the coolness of trees and there would be fresh grass for you to eat. Perhaps you could escape, run and be free."

"Maa," Daisy butted her wooden enclosure as if trying to get out to me.

"I'm sorry," I said. "Pansy, the two of you take care of each other. You are my dear little friends."

As I left I could hear their voices, calling and calling but I could not go back.

I knew the way to my father's quarters.

The door hung open but despite that the cabin was filled with the sickening smell of Herc. Clothes, torn and foul, spilled from a canvas bag on the floor. The bunk where my father had slept was covered by a patchwork quilt that might once have been on an elegant bed on some fancy plundered ship. Now it was stained and torn.

On the dresser was what I had come for, the silver brush that had once been my mother's. How often I had seen her sit by her mirror in our home, brushing her long brown hair, twisting it up with a ribbon. She had given it to my father when he left on one of his long voyages. I swallowed back tears and picked up the brush. Strands of Herc's hair clung to it. He had been using it. I shivered with distaste but stuffed it in my pocket then opened the cupboard door to peer into its blackness. At first I saw nothing. Then, as my eyes grew accustomed to the lack of light I saw clothing that must have been Herc's hanging on pegs. A red shiny coat, elephant size, with buttons missing; a pair of red britches buckled at the knee, soiled and smelly; stockings that had once been white dangling from the same peg. I slid past them. My father's hat with the feather was still on the shelf. It had been pushed to the back along with a pair of velvet slippers, a vest with silver buttons and a sword in a black scabbard adorned with jewels which by their very size told me they were tawdry and false. My father's velvet coat was crumpled on the floor along with some other clothing. My foot touched something soft and yielding and I immediately knew what it was. My mother's petticoat, the one my father had carried with him on all of his voyages to remind him of her. She had worn it on their honeymoon. I wished I had known of its existence before she died. If I had I would have asked my father to have it buried with her, but he would have been loath to give it up, this dear memory of her. I held it to my face and smelled the faint flower scent that still clung to it after all these years. Then I rolled it small and slid it under my shirt.

Someone was coming.

I froze, uncertain if I should scurry back into the cupboard and stay hidden.

It was William. "I knew you'd be here," he said.

I took a step toward him and he closed the cabin door. We looked at each other and there was a shyness between us, an air charged with expectation. We had clung together for a few dangerous moments on the deck of the *Sea Wolf*, but this was different. The cabin door was closed. We were truly alone as we had been on Pox Island.

I tried to speak but when I did the words I spoke were of no importance. "A captain's door must always remain open," I stammered and William smiled.

"Aye."

There was no need to speak again.

We clung to each other as if there had been no time between now and the days and nights we'd spent together on the sands of the island. I breathed in the smell of his skin so well remembered.

"I love the softness of ye," he murmured.

We stood apart, gazing at each other and he lifted one of my hands to his lips, then stopped. "Oh me love, your poor fingers. Is it from the sail needle?"

I nodded.

One by one he kissed them, whispers of kisses that made me weak.

"But what, what is this? Something in your pocket?"

"My mother's silver brush," I said, half smiling, half weeping.

"And this?" He answered himself. "The flute. Our savior. What else have ye got, tucked into yerself?" He pulled the silken petticoat from beneath my shirt.

"It was my mother's," I said. "I want to keep it forever and ever."

"I will keep it for ye, forever and ever," William said. "Ye will wear it for me when we are wed."

"My mother would like that, her daughter wedded to the man she loves, wearing what she wore for my father."

He pushed the petticoat inside his shirt and I thought, Now it will smell of my mother and of him. I was no longer aware of the lingering presence of Herc in the cabin, nor of the grate and slide of the barrels on the deck above, or the raucous shouts of the men, or the slide and lurch of the damaged ship. There was only William.

His lips on mine, his sweet words in my ears. "I love ye so. I loved ye before I knew ye."

"Wait!" I heard footsteps and slid from his arms. Someone else was coming. I had to hide. Back in the cupboard! I stumbled into its darkness, pulled the door closed.

"William!" Captain Moriarity's voice.

I clenched my fists. If she found me here, with William, it would be a flogging for me, if not for him. Or an island. It could even be an island.

"This is where I come upon ye, William," she said. "You were not on deck wi' the rest of the men. Are ye discoverin' aught good in his cabin that ye could take for yerself?"

She looked around. "Dog's blood! Is this the cabin of a captain? It is more like the den of a wild boar."

I found the crack in the cupboard door. I had used this cupboard, this crack, once before to spy on Herc and Hopper when they had been secretly searching for the Burmese Sunrise. Now I could see little for William had placed himself between the captain and my hiding place. She was speaking.

"I had the need to find ye," she said.

"You have been injured yerself, Cap'n," William said, easing away from the danger in her words. "Ye must have the carpenter here look at your arm. He's good at sewin' up a gash."

I listened to the silence outside my cupboard. William's back was still in the way of my seeing. He hadn't moved then. He had not gone to her. I held my breath, as if something of great portent was about to happen. Was the captain going to give voice to her feelings for William? I closed my eyes. Please, no, I thought. I cannot bear to hear her say the words. But hear I will if she speaks. There is no escape.

"I am going to tell you what I have told no person before," the captain said. "Considering the insinuations that putrid cap'n let fall. God rest him."

William spoke quickly. "No need to tell me aught,

Cap'n. I pay no mind to what that maggot says." He stopped and added, "God rest him."

I knew myself to be listening with my body tensed, my throat dry as bran.

"I was your age once," the captain said. "Younger, even. I had a love."

There was another silence. To me, the silences were worse than the words.

"Do ye want to be tellin' me this?" I detected an apprehension in William's tone. He was captive, as I was.

"My love had yellow hair, same as yours, the color o' sunshine, soft as silk." Her voice was hoarse. She moved a little and now I could see her plainly. The wild red mane blazed. Blood trickled from her arm, dripped from the hand that shaded her eyes. And her face, her face was different. It was twisted out of shape, angry, anguished.

"I was fourteen years of age and full of fire and pride. Oh yes, I had pride. I was sailing on the *Sea Wolf,* my father's ship, and Henry was workin' wi' the carpenter on the brig, *Calliope.* I'd asked my father and he gave me leave to invite him to come sail wi' us instead. We came into port a day early for stores and I went lookin' for my love. To tell him we could be together forever. I found him and I made to run to him, but he was busy. Busy with a wench with hair as black as night that hung like a shawl down her back. They was kissin' and laughin' and I cursed the two o' them with every evil thought in me mind and I ran back on me father's ship, me heart broken."

I felt unsteady and I leaned against the wall of the cupboard, against Herc's malodorous coat. The small movement set it to swinging and I tensed. What if she flung open the door and found me cowering here? But she was talking again in that raspy voice.

"We sailed the next day and I had time on that cruise to savor my anger and then my remorse. And devour my wicked pride. I reminded meself that seamen chase women when they gets time to disport theirselves in port. 'Twas me he loved. She was an amusement, nothing more. I remembered moments wi' him." She stopped. "Even now those moments torment me heart. I tried to find him again. I never did. I have mourned me loss since that cursed day."

More silence. Above us I could hear the tramp of feet, the thump of boxes thrown around. A loud voice called. "Keep a grip on that cask, ye son of an English billy goat" and an answering yell, "Hold yer water. I'm a holdin' it."

I saw her move closer to William. "He would be older 'n you now, William. He would be more than twenty, like meself. I did not even take a clipping' o' his hair. It gave me a turn when I first laid eyes on you. I thought I had seen a ghost. 'Twas me own guilt and heartbreak I saw starin' at me wi' his blue eyes."

" 'Tis useless to blame yerself," William said. " 'Tis over and done."

I saw his eyes flicker to the cupboard where I crouched and then flicker away.

"Never over and never done," she said and I saw her lay her blooded hand on William's arm. "Now I have a second chance. Now there is you. Will ye sail wi' me? Will ye help me atone for the love I lost and willfully tossed away? I know we be's different ages, but ye will grow older and I will stay the same. That is how it works. You will see. I believe I have twenty-six years now, or mayhap twenty-seven. Do not have a care about that. We will live our lives happily together. William?" her voice softened, became a lullaby. "Half of all I have, half of the *Sea Wolf* will be yours."

I leaned again against Herc's vile coat, even held a sleeve of it to cover my eyes. I could not bear this.

"There is Catherine," William said. "I will love her forever. That will not change."

" 'Tis a childish thing, the way ye think on her. 'Twill pass."

"Ye want me to leave her? The way ye left him?"

"Ye cannot have her with ye. I will give my word that

she will have safe passage back to where she came from. On this voyage and others I will instruct ye on the workings of my ship... our ship. We will own it together. 'Twill be yer future, William, and a goodly one."

I pressed my nails into my palms. They were already painful from the sail needle and I felt them cut my skin. If I went out now and confronted the she-wolf, it would be the end of me. There would be no taking me back to Port Teresa. I would be thrown overboard or put off on one of the islands that haunted my nightmares. This was the woman who had killed Herc only because he provoked her. Intended or not, she had not hesitated. She would not hesitate to get rid of me if it suited her purpose.

"Well, do ye have an answer to me invitation?" The captain's voice was almost teasing. I could tell she had no doubt as to William's decision. I knew he would not say "yes" to her. Not my William! He would never abandon me like that. But... to be part owner of a ship like the *Sea Wolf?*

This silence between them was long.

I waited.

At last William answered.

"I will think on it," he said.

Chapter Thirteen

The captain and William left together.

William did not cast a glance at the cupboard and I told myself that it was because he did not wish to draw attention to my hiding place.

I came out into the cabin, the floor of which was tilted to port. My father's hat on the shelf, Herc's boots, his scabbard had slithered together in a jumble at the back of the cupboard. My legs shook. My mind turned over and over the words I had heard her speak. And his response. "I will think on it." I would have preferred that he deny her immediately. But that might not have been wise.

The thrashing and smashing from the deck above had become more strident. They have found rum or brandy, I thought, and are already sampling it. I knew some of them would fall from the rope into the sea and be fished out with much laughter and catcalling. They would lie on the deck, singing and drinking till daybreak.

Whatever happens, I must find William.

I struggled back across the rope to the *Sea Wolf*. Skelly was in front of me. He turned his head and asked, "Are you unhurt, Mistress?"

"Yes," I said. Unhurt outside, bleeding inside.

" 'Tis hard for ye, yer father's ship," he said.

I swallowed. "Very hard." One of the lenses of his eyepiece was cracked and spiderwebbed across the glass. I felt a rush of gratitude for him, for his concern and kindness toward me from the time he first saw me.

It was he who helped me scramble back aboard the *Sea Wolf* now. I looked along the crowded deck. The celebrations had started and some of the men were already in their cups.

Where was William?

I saw him then. He was in the wheelhouse with Captain Moriarity. She is already teaching him the workings of the ship, I thought. There would likely be no written instructions that she would need to read. She had known this ship and these waters for many years. That information she would pass on to William, the one with whom she wanted to share her life. In the cabin he had spoken again of his love for me, he had kissed me, he had pledged himself. He had told the captain that he would love me forever. I drew strength from the memory. Did he still have my mother's petticoat pressed against his body?

Sebastian was not seated by the sails but I sat and picked up the needle. I had difficulty seeing but I persisted, glad of the pain in my fingers, glad of the pricks of blood that dotted them. The pain removed the anguish in my mind. He had kissed them, these poor ugly fingers, pressing them to his lips one at a time.

Sebastian came staggering along the deck and squirreled down beside me. "Aye, 'twas a grand fight," he said with much satisfaction. "It exercises the muscles and then the rum soothes them. 'Tis a good arrangement."

I nodded without answering.

The ship lay at rest on the ocean. The sails hung empty, relieved of their work. But there was pandemonium around us. Rum flowed. Someone had poured or spilled brandy on the deck. It smelled, but not unpleasantly.

Now and then Sebastian scrambled out from under the sail and refilled his mug with rum. I could not see from where I sat if William and the captain were still together and I could not decide if it was better to know or to wonder.

But then I saw her, alone, walking along the deck, threading her way among the drunken crew. She laughed along with them, accepted a drink from a cup that Frenchy presented to her, ran her hands merrily through her hair, so that it stood up like a burning bush. On her injured hand was a rough wrap. Who had tied it there? William?

"Cap'n be's happy," Sebastian said. "That's always her way after a battle. It makes her flourish, like."

"Aye." That and other matters, I thought.

She was addressing the crew.

"Listen now, ye belly-whackers," she said. "Drink yer fill. Enjoy yer success. But the morrow it's back to work. We'll be underway afore sunrise. One more day wi' the wind right and we'll spot the *Isabella*. Then there'll be a glittering treasure, ye can lay to that."

I needed to be alone, away from the deck and the men of the *Sea Wolf*.

"I do not feel well," I told Sebastian. It was not altogether true but it was a reasonable excuse to leave.

"Have a swig o' this." Sebastian offered me the cup. "It'll warm yer blood and rattle yer bones."

"Thank you, but I had better go."

I made my unsteady way to the captain's cabin.

My mother's brush was still in my pocket. I took it out, pulled the strands of Herc's horrible hair from the bristles, then lay in my hammock, thinking wandering thoughts. If I were a good person I would want William to stay with Captain Moriarity. He would have a life, better than the one with me.

Somehow I must see him and ask what he had decided. Perhaps he would feel it was wiser to appear to agree to her request until we had a chance to escape together. Whatever his plan I had to know. I would seize any opportunity, however dangerous, that came my way to meet with him.

I feigned sleep when at last the captain came to the cabin. There would be no reading tonight. Through lidded eyes I watched her make her usual preparations for sleep. I watched her take the lock of hair from the box and hold it between her steepled hands as if she were praying. I saw her smile and I lay stiff and miserable in the hammock. She must have been imbibing steadily herself for she bumped into the leg of the throne chair and swore loudly when she sloshed water over the top of the washbowl.

She took off all her clothes and stood considering the bowl of water that Gummer had left. I had not seen her naked before and I could not help but admire the long, strong limbs and smooth back. Medb, queen of the pirates, beautiful and splendid. It was difficult to believe that she was as old as she had confessed to being. It did not matter. The heart-wrenching thought came. It would not matter to William. "Ye will come," she'd promised him.

She moved and I closed my eyes quickly lest she catch me intruding on her privacy.

She dried herself with a torn shirt, and began pulling her canvas trousers on again, favoring her bandaged arm. Through my half-closed eyes I was aware of how difficult it was for her to step into the trousers. She hopped on one foot, clutched at the arm of the chair and finally sat to pull the trousers all the way up.

Slowly and carefully she made her way to the door, laid her hands on the painted cross, muttered the prayer or whatever the words were she spoke, and staggered back to her bed. She forgot to shutter the lamp.

My heart began to beat so fast it was ready to leap from my chest.

She had forgotten to lock the door.

Soon I heard her snores, fulsome and loud where on other nights they had been gentle.

I slipped out of my hammock and crouched beside it.

Seize the chance, I told myself. Do not let it get away from you.

There were still boisterous noises from the deck but I thought they were less forceful. Many would be already drunkenly asleep.

The *Sea Wolf* drowsed, hushed by the sea beneath her. The light from the lantern cast moving shadows that drifted with the ship, lighting her face, moving across my empty hammock.

I pulled on my canvas shoes, slid my knife into the band of my pantaloons and crossed the cabin on tiptoe. In the bundle of clothing I'd gotten from Mr. Forthinggale I remembered a cap. It smelled of grease but it would do. My hair had grown since the day I had hacked it off with my mother's sewing scissors, standing in the kitchen at home, wanting to be taken for a boy and a pirate. Now it curled over my ears. I pulled the cap down to hide it then stealthily made my way to the door. I touched the cross for whatever reason and turned the handle.

The three-quarter moon gave a pale light. The crew lay, some spread eagled, loose limbed. Some had propped themselves against bulkheads, some were yet half awake, mumbling to themselves, still holding the mugs of rum they had brought from the *Reprisal*. None stirred as I passed.

Where was William?

There were dark blotches on the boards of the deck,

either spilled rum or the urine of men too drunk or too lazy to go to the railing to relieve themselves. There was vomit and globs of spit. The smells made me gag. I tried to avoid stepping in something I did not want to step in.

One man, I thought it was Jenks, sang softly. "Joe Jelly fought a shark, he fought a shark and ate its belly," he sang. "The shark weren't dead, Joe thought it was...." The voice tapered to a mumble.

There was a gap in the railing and splinters of wood peppered the deck. One of the *Reprisal*'s shells had found its mark. I could see the ocean through a small hole in the hull above the waterline. There would be patching to be done.

The moon silvered the sea, moving gently up and down in the sky in tune with the *Sea Wolf*'s small motion. In the far distance I saw a shape, low in the water listing heavily to starboard. The *Reprisal*, carrying her dead captain, looking for a friendly cove to careen herself and make repairs. My father's ship, and still afloat.

But where was William?

I looked for the glint of his hair, gilded by moonlight and saw it. He was asleep in a hammock slung between two cannons. My heart filled with relief and I spoke his name but a hand, coming from nowhere, grasped my ankle and pulled me down with a thump onto the deck. A scream rose in my throat but I squeezed it back. I must not draw attention to myself.

I struggled, my heels thumping on the deck, my arms pulled painfully behind my back.

"Aye. I thought 'twas you," a drunken voice said. "I know the walk o' ye for I've watched ye plenty."

Magruder! Magruder, whose lecherous glances and whispered suggestions had tormented me all through the voyage.

I butted with my head against his chest, which was matted with something damp and sticky. Rum maybe, or blood.

"Lookin' for a little lovin'?" he asked. "I came callin' on ye one night but ye didn't open the door. Bad cess to the cap'n. She had ye locked in." He belched a malodorous belch.

Though he was intoxicated I could tell he was not incapacitated. There was strength in the arms that trapped me, in the legs that clutched around mine. I felt I had lived through this before, on the *Reprisal* with Herc, drunk too, and filled with lust. William saving me.

Magruder was under me and I was pressed against him, my arms twisted behind my back. His foul breath wheezed in my face. Without another thought I leaned over and with every bit of strength in me bit down on his pointed nose. It was in my mouth. I clenched my teeth on it and felt it, slippery, nauseating. Disgusting slime bubbled through it, as he yelped his pain and every instinct I had told me to let go, to spit out what was oozing into my mouth, but I held on.

"Let go! I'll tear yer heart out." His voice was hollow, like an echo. He loosened his grip to shove at my shoulders and I pulled the knife from under my shirt and put it to his throat.

It took all the stamina I had left to get to my feet, the knife still shining in my hand.

Magruder groaned and rolled over on the deck. He got to his knees, then his feet. "I'm bleedin', ye vixen," he snorted, blowing his nose violently onto the deck.

I backed away. I'd seen William, in that second before Magruder grabbed me. He was here somewhere, close, in a hammock.

I saw him then and I took hold of the edge of the hammock in which he lay and almost turned it over. "William, William," I whispered.

"Catherine?" He was awake at once. "Is this you? What is it? What are ye doin' here?" He was standing now, standing in front of me.

"I came to find you. Magruder..."

"She near mangled me nose. She took a knife to me.

She'll pay for this. I'll see to it she gets the cat. She'll..." Magruder lurched at me but William pushed me behind him.

"Aye, Magruder," he said. "Ye'll be the laughin' stock o' the ship. Magruder got bested by a woman. He couldn't handle her. He never could hold on to a woman. That milksop! That worm."

"Shut yer mouth," Magruder said.

Even in the weak moonshine I could see the trickle of blood running from his nose onto his chin.

"Ye'd do well to tell 'em you got yer nose sliced in the battle, when ye were fightin' like a man," William said and all the time he was easing me away. And all the time I was pushing around him to get back at Magruder.

"Leave be, Catherine," William said. "Ye've done enough. I do not think he will talk. He is too prideful to be mocked. Are ye all right, me love."

"Yes," I whispered. Strangely my cap was still on my head and I pushed the straggles of hair back under it.

"What made ye take such a chance, Catherine?" William murmured.

"I had to know," I whispered. "Is it to be her or me? I heard how she talked, in the cabin." My legs were suddenly weak and if it were not for William's arm I would have fallen.

"Who be's there?" someone called, someone drunk who weaved about in front of us.

"Nobody." William pushed the man away. "Go back to sleep." He leaned down to me, his mouth against my ear. "Ye must go, Catherine. Go before something worse happens. Can ye walk? I'll take ye."

"No." I spoke around the dryness in my throat. "Better I go myself. But have you given her your answer?"

"Not yet," he said. "I have to think on what's best to do. She has promised ye safe passage back to Port Teresa. She will not maroon ye, no matter how ye provoke her. Ye will be safe."

And then someone else, someone small and short-legged took my arm. "I'll see to her," Sebastian said and he led me in silence back to the captain's cabin.

Chapter Fourteen

I lay in the hammock listening to Captain Moriarity's loud snores, trying to think. I had gone to ask William what his decision was to be and I'd found no answer. "I have to think what's best to do." Best for me? To ensure my safe passage back to Port Teresa? Yes. But was there more? I knew him. I loved him. But I could not ignore the doubt that crept into my mind. Which course would he take?

The lamp, still lit, was guttering, most likely from lack of oil. I held my mother's hairbrush close to my heart and tried to think.

My mind turned to what had happened tonight. Would Magruder tell?

Lying, sleepless in the half dark, I waited for sunrise.

When the first light showed itself in the cabin I heard the captain arise. "Get ye up, mistress. Sebastian will be waitin'. Don't ye be lollygaggin'."

She sounded well pleased by something. I did not care to know what.

I arose quickly and went on deck.

The sun was lifting itself, red between sky and sea. The *Sea Wolf* was underway, her sails full throated, her bow rising and falling, the mermaid on the prow dipping and lifting, dipping and lifting, showering the deck with spray. The sheets whipped against the masts. One day more and we would see the *Isabella*.

There was commotion all around and the strong smell of vinegar as the men washed down the decks to cleanse them from last night's filth.

Repairs to the hull had started. Even going into another battle the *Sea Wolf* must be kept shipshape.

The morning held a sense of excitement, an urgency. It was as if the men, who had been drunk and enfeebled last night, had come alive and could feel the prize they had come so far to take. They smelled gold and jewels. Sails were manipulated to better catch the wind.

Almost there. Almost there.

Yesterday they had had a taste of blood and booty

and they craved more.

Sebastian was already at work. I slid my legs under the sail beside him and picked up my needle. His face was ill humored, and I suspected that he was suffering from too much rum last night. He made no mention of what had transpired and how he had walked with me to the captain's cabin. I kept my own counsel.

There was no sign of William. Was he already with the captain or had she put him to work, far from where I sewed?

I was about to try an opening conversation with Sebastian when I saw Magruder. He strode past us. His nose had swollen like a bap and dried blood caked the nostrils. On either side of it I could see puncture wounds where my teeth had gripped him.

Sebastian stopped sewing and bent forward, watching him.

"He be's headed for the wheelhouse," he said. "I'll wager he wants an audience wi' the captain." He glanced at me sideways. "He be's a weasel, that 'un. Tellin' her a tale, no doubt."

The tone of his voice told me he knew what tale Magruder would likely be telling. My heart plunged. I knew, too.

I sat, blindly plying the sail needle, waiting for her wrath to consume me.

It was not long in coming.

One look at the captain as she strode along the deck told me that she had heard the tale and was infuriated. Her lips were pulled together in a tight line. Her fists were clenched at her sides. Magruder paced behind her, a few steps back, grinning an idiotic grin. A hammer lay on the deck and the captain kicked it away with an oath and a bellow.

"Which o' ye slovenly pigs left this a'lyin for me to trip over? Pick it up."

It was the pirate I called Bandit who made haste to retrieve it.

I bent my head and pretended to sew. If only she would walk past. But I knew she would not.

The feet came closer and closer. Stopped.

"Get up, wench!"

I lifted the edge of the sail from my legs and stood. My heart pounded in my ears.

She stood in front of me, her hands on her hips. Her eyes were red, the way they had been the first time I saw her.

Behind her Magruder waited, delicately fingering his nose.

"Is it true ye defied me orders and went by night to be wi' William?" she asked.

Sebastian scrambled up and the men who had been working close to us lessened their efforts so they could listen to what was happening.

"Well, is it true?"

Before I could answer, or think about answering, the captain reached behind her and dragged Magruder forward.

"Aye, 'tis true," Magruder said.

"Magruder tried to stop ye from breakin' my rules and ye bit him. See here on his snout? Ye were goin' to kill him but for William coming upon the scene and draggin' ye away. Do not deny it for I see the proof of it in yer face. Ye disregarded me spoken orders. Is this the thanks yer givin' me for pluckin' ye off Pox Island?"

"I do thank you," I said. "Did Magruder tell you he tried to catch hold of me in an obnoxious way? That I was defending..."

Captain Moriarity raised a fist. "Do not speak another word ye treacherous vixen. Ye were where ye should not have been. Ye stole the key to the door."

"I did not," I said. "You left the door unlocked. I wanted only..."

A small crowd had gathered, watching expectantly. And then I saw William. He shouldered through the others to get to me.

"Cap'n," he began. " 'Twas my fault, too."

"No," the captain said. " 'Twas not yer fault. The besom came to you. All ye did was save Magruder from her knife. She broke me rules. She shall be punished. I have not decided on it yet, but 'twill be just and severe, you can lay to that."

"We did not touch. We scarce spoke," William began.

"I need hear no more." Her voice was sharp and full of anger.

"Ye promised her safe passage," William said.

"Aye. And she will have it, if'n ye meet me conditions."

Her conditions? She meant if William promised to stay with her and leave me.

"I did not attest to her comfort on her return journey," the captain went on. "Be warned! I do not deal lightly with those who go against me."

There was a muttering from the hovering crew.

"Cap'n," one of them shouted. "We be's wasting time. Attend to the wench after."

"Aye. Let her be for now. The *Sea Wolf* has pressin' business. Treasure business." That was Gabby, a piece of broken railing in his hand.

The captain's glance swept over the men. "You are right. All of yez get to work. Go! Go!"

They scattered quickly. She pointed at Magruder.

"You! Wait! 'Twas your snout she bit on. 'Twill be yer pleasure to take the hussy down and lock her in the brig. I'll see to her later. And William. You will fight alongside us. I will have need of every man when we meet up with the *Isabella*."

"Beg pardon, Cap'n." That was Sebastian in an ingratiating voice I had never yet heard him use. "I understands yer position. But I have use for the wench. She be's quick wi' the needle. Should we lose our sails to an *Isabella* cannonball we will want this topsail. She and I be's workin' hard on it for 'tis bad tore."

Captain Moriarity grunted. "She will be in the brig tonight then. She'll be in your charge today, Sebastian, and I caution ye not to go easy on her."

William's lips touched my hair, such a whisper of a touch that I might have imagined it.

I wanted to whimper, to beg, to grovel. How could I survive a black night in the brig, in the bowels of the ship, with only my own dark thoughts and fears?

"I'll take her place," William said. "Let me go and..."

"Ye will do no such an' a thing. Of what use would that be to punish her?"

" 'Twould keep us from each other, Cap'n. She would not be tryin' to come to me."

"Do not speak!" The captain's mouth was a tight line.

"When the sun goes down, she goes in the brig and that is me order."

Sebastian stood directly in front of the captain. "Cap'n? I beg leave to talk with ye."

"Aye. Talk away. You, girl, get back to the sewin' on that sail that's makin' Sebastian anxious."

Sebastian waited till I was seated before he spoke again. I was supposed to not hear but I strained and caught hold of some of his words.

"This mornin' as I was… along the deck before sunrise I saw a horrible…"

I had missed two words.

"Aye? Ye saw what?"

"The horseshoe on the mast had turned… It was upside down. I fear it has thrown out… I righted it, Cap'n. Mayhap I got to it afore all its luck had emptied."

I kept my head bent over my needle but a quick glance showed me how the captain leaned forward, her eyes fixed on Sebastian's face.

He swayed from side to side, steadying himself against the movement of the ship. For a moment there was silence and I thought I had missed more of his talk, but then he said, "Below it, Cap'n, where the luck had scattered…" He stopped again.

"Somethin' there."

"Satan's tooth, Sebastian. Stop shilly-shallying." Her voice was raised and shrill. "What was there?"

"A rat, Cap'n. A big 'un. Black, wi' eyes as red as yer own. Beggin' yer pardon." His tone was measured and I heard it clearly.

The captain shuffled and looked down as if expecting to see the rat at her feet. "I do not like rats," she said. "'Twas a bold one to be out so... and lettin' you..." The rest of what she spoke was uttered so low that I could not catch it.

I shivered. A rat! I was not fond of rats either and this picture of one with red eyes was fearsome to me.

"Aye, and there's more," Sebastian went on. "Catman's cat came round the... up there by the fo'c's'le, and the rat seen it and he turned tail and ran, an' he was screechin' like the devil. I stomped my foot... go too near him and then..."

I scraped myself along a little, getting closer to them, the better to hear. But they had forgotten I was hard by.

"And then?"

Uneasy bumps rose on my arms. There was something terrifying in this conversation, but I kept my needle busy. I had to be seen to be working hard, justifying Sebastian's need of me.

"And then I saw what we's been fearin'." Sebastian glanced at me where I sat and I let my shoulders slump in a disinterested way. The captain disregarded me, her whole body intent on Sebastian. "It was HER?" she asked. "The witch? The malevolent spirit?"

"Aye. I saw it plain. 'Twas HER."

The captain touched her lips, made a small sound.

I allowed myself to look up, keeping my expression uninvolved.

"What can we do?" Captain Moriarity asked.

"Nothing that I knows of. SHE sensed my presence and before I could... to do aught, startled as I was, SHE scurried through the... and down below decks. I am sorry, Cap'n."

"SHE, the evil one, is still aboard?"

"Aye. Far as I knows."

I sat, trying to make sense of what I heard. They were talking about HER again, the unknown SHE that had made the captain inspect every one of the men.

"We will keep this from the crew," the captain said. "There is no need to vex them."

There was a sudden crash. I jumped to my feet.

"What...?" The captain and Sebastian spun around and I peered over Sebastian's shoulder. The polished wood with the words Bonne Chance carved into it had fallen from its place above the door and lay facedown on the deck.

"Holy Heaven," the captain breathed. Her face had paled. "What does it all portend?"

"The omens are averse, Cap'n. Ye knows I always have yer best interests in mind and I would only advise ye on what is evident. The black rat is death, and now that SHE has taken it over it is beyond evil. I beg ye to abandon yer attack on the *Isabella*."

The captain's glance flickered around the deck, landed on me where I stood not far from them.

"Get ye away, girl! There's nothin' of interest to ye here." She did not wait to see if I obeyed. "Sebastian! Pick up the Bonne Chance, and put it in a safe place till we have completed our battle. And there is to be no mention of the rat or HER. I tell ye true, I am frightened. But I will not abandon the skirmish. The men would surely wreck me ship if'n I stopped them from this venture when they have come so far. They may respect me but they are not a forgiving group. God's Bones! I am uneasy at leaving HER on board. Mayhap the roar of the cannons and the stink of the gunfire will scare her off."

Sebastian did not answer.

"Mayhap SHE will desert us and go to the *Isabella*," the captain went on and it was as if she was trying to persuade herself. "If SHE does not leave we will have to find her and destroy her."

" 'Twill be hard, Cap'n. None of the men will want to take part in that hunt. Not when they are told what SHE be's."

The captain scratched under the rag that bound her hand. "We will face that at a later time. For now we must take all measures we know of to make good luck for ourselves."

"Aye. We'll do what we can. But I fear 'twill not be enough. Not with HER on board to see to it that we do not succeed."

The captain gave Sebastian a baleful stare then strode away along the deck, calling out orders to her crew.

Sebastian sighed heavily and sat down next to me.

I looked up at the grimness of his expression and then I glanced nervously at the sea. My heart jittered in my chest. The sun was dipping down into the ocean. How much longer before it set? The brig. The rat with red eyes below decks. I had to speak, to break this silence between us.

"Could you tell me now what is taking place?" I asked. "I heard a lot of what was said and I am mystified."

"Cap'n would not like to have you told. I attend always to her wishes. But this time, I think it right that you should know. SHE could be a danger to ye, and ye down there in the brig. We have a witch on board. SHE came, sailing out to us on an eggshell and climbed the rope. SHE has now taken over the body of the black rat. We feared SHE might have entered one of the crew, or you, or William. But your auras were clear. I was able to reassure Cap'n on all of the crew. I read the auras, the spirit color that rises from a body. The rat's aura was black, the color of herself, the color of HER. The color of death."

I had stopped in the act of threading my needle to stare at him. "A witch? Coming in an eggshell?" I gave a short, nervous laugh. "Sebastian! You cannot believe such a thing."

"I do believe, Mistress, and you should too." I could tell my words had annoyed him so I made sure to listen with full attention.

"Witches be's the enemies of sailing vessels," he said. "They stir up storms, cause destruction, deal out death. 'Tis their pleasure and skill."

"You saw her come in an eggshell?" I asked, making sure to speak politely. "But how did she fit in it?"

"SHE is a witch. She can make herself any size, small enough to enter a rat. I did not see HER but I saw the empty eggshell, floating by our ship, way out here in the middle of the sea." He shuddered. "A witch that came to the *Vengeance*, a brig my cousin sailed on, blew up a fog so bad they ran aground on a shoal and near foundered.

'Twas by good fortune they did not all drown. But they lost three men, God rest them. And they found the dead finger o' one, after, in an eggshell that floated by their ship."

I sat, incredulous. How could this be true? I shuffled a little closer to Sebastian. "But SHE, this witch, has done nothing to the *Sea Wolf* or to the crew," I said.

Sebastian made a sign in the air with his two fingers as if to ward off evil. "Not yet," he said.

Chapter Fifteen

The sun had set. The sky was crimson where it had been.

Magruder came strutting along the deck to where I sat with the sail, pretending I had not noticed that the day was ending.

"Get up, ye strumpet!" he said. " 'Tis sundown and you and me, we has business together." He grabbed ahold of my arm and I twisted my wrist so the sail needle stuck into his hand.

He let go of me.

"God's blood!" he yelled, "Ye pierced me, ye she-devil!" He sucked at the puncture that was already oozing. His other hand seized a handful of my hair. "On yer feet," he hissed, but Sebastian was scrabbling up beside me.

"Let go o' her. I needs to leave and talk to the cap'n. Do not touch Mistress Catherine again till I get back or ye'll answer to me."

⚓

Sebastian was gone, leaving me to rub my scalp, which was shot through with pain, leaving Magruder to suck on his hand, his hate-filled eyes fixed on me.

In a few minutes Sebastian was back.

"The girl is not to be taken to the brig. Not this night, on command o' the cap'n."

"The cap'n said? Ye're sure about that? What changed her thinkin'? And am I to believe ye?"

"Ye doubt me word?" Sebastian glared up at Magruder. "As to what the cap'n be's thinkin', 'tis not for the likes o' ye to know. Get ye back to what ye were doin'. We've seen enough o' ye."

Magruder went, casting malicious glances back in our direction.

"He's put out," Sebastian said. "No doubt he had other plans for you and him on the way down to the brig."

I stumbled to my feet. "Thank ye, Sebastian. Whatever..."

He held up a key. "I'm to lock ye in the cap'n's cabin

and gi' her back the key. Ye're to have no dinner and I'm sorry ye be's missin' out on it. Pig's liver. We always eats good on the night afore a battle."

I took a deep breath. "I care nothing about that. How did you convince her?"

"I told her the truth. I told her the witch could get to ye down there. The witch knows right well ye be's at odds wi' the cap'n. Knows ye might be willin' to aid HER. The devil hisself would never be certain what SHE'd put ye up to."

I did not know if his speculation was true or part of his own superstition. "Thank you," I said again.

He nodded "We'd best go."

I was almost glad when I heard him turn the key in the lock so I was alone in the cabin, with the brig and today's anxieties shut outside. But the anxieties lay in wait to frighten my mind.

Gummer had already lighted the lantern.

I took William Shakespeare's *As You Like It* from the bookshelf, sat in the throne chair and tried to read.

Sweet are the uses of adversity,
Which, like the toad, ugly and venomous,
Wears yet a precious jewel in his head.

Was this truth? I could find no use for the adversity in which I found myself.

I read on. Always I could lose myself in reading, but tonight was different. The words made little sense.

I closed the book and put it back in its place.

I needed my flute.

Softly I played, the sweetness of the notes rising around me, easing my heart. The song my mother had loved best. I had so many memories. The way we'd walk together on the beach, gathering the shells and pebbles as we went. Her excitement when she found a sand dollar. "Look, Catherine, a little sea creature once lived in this ivory palace." How long ago it seemed since we'd walked together. How long since I'd played for her. How far away her resting place on Cobb Hill. Tears choked my throat.

Around me the timbers creaked. Through the porthole I could see a dark flurry of sky.

I did not know how much time passed before I roused myself.

I used the commode, unable to go tonight to the stern. I washed in the basin Gummer had left filled with fresh water for the captain and squirmed into my hammock. Sleep was far from me.

Where was William?

When I heard his voice, soft outside, I thought I was imagining it.

"Catherine? I'm here me love."

I rushed to the locked door. "William! I cannot believe it is you! If only I hadn't acted so foolishly, going to you. I am thankful that she is not punishing you, though I know she never would."

There was a silence. Then I asked. "Do you know what else she has in mind for me?"

"She will do nothin' till we have engaged with the *Isabella*. That is uppermost in her mind. Try to endure, me love. Think on good things. How 'twill be when this is over."

I stood with my hand on the Celtic cross, straining to hear him, wanting with all my heart to believe.

"She is coming." His voice was urgent. "Go from the door. Hurry."

I did not wait a second longer but swung back into the hammock, pretending sleep.

I heard the key turn and the door swing open.

Another minute. "God's breath, wench! Ye provoke me. Ye've used me commode and sullied me washin' water."

I did not respond. Wasn't I asleep?

I heard her perform her rituals and the screak of her bed.

We lay together in a cabin of silence. Outside the sea slid quietly past the *Sea Wolf* while the sails caught what night wind they could, and the stars circled above. We lay awake while the lookout, awake too and alert, watched for obstacles in the sea or for a first happy sighting of the *Isabella*. While down below, skulking in some dark corner if I believed Sebastian, the black rat of death waited.

The captain sighed and turned heavily in her bunk. She got up after some time, went to the door to touch the cross and spoke. "Protect me, protect me ship, protect me men." There was a pause and then she whispered, "Protect William." She crossed the cabin and slid again below her blanket. Sebastian's warning must be troubling her mind, I thought, though she had tried to dismiss it.

I coughed. "Captain?"

She did not acknowledge me.

"Captain, I know you are awake. I am sorry to interrupt your thinking but I beg leave to speak of something of great importance."

"You have naught of import to say to me."

I formed the words I would say.

"I have a jewel," I hurried on before she could stop me. "It is called the Burmese Sunrise."

I sensed an attentiveness, a listening. Had the captain heard of the Burmese Sunrise? Did she know its value?

"It is in my possession, hidden in a place no one knows but me." William also knew, but that I would not reveal. "It is worth more than any one jewel you will find on the *Isabella*," I went on, "though I know there will be other treasures awaiting on you aboard the ship. The Burmese Sunrise is a ruby, big as a lark's egg, filled with fire enough to hurt your eyes and the diamonds that border it blaze brighter than the Milky Way. I was told it once belonged to an Indian sultan before it was gifted to my father by a grateful captain whose life he spared."

I waited anxiously for her to speak but she did not.

"I swear to you that on the soul of my dead mother and the honor of my dear, dead father I shall give it to you if you do not put me in the brig and if you return William and me, together and unharmed, to Port Teresa. I know you have promised safe voyage to me, but it would mean little to me if he were not with me."

"Silence!" The word was loud and vicious as a pistol shot. "Ye dare to bargain wi' me, ye miserable besom? If I want to discover the whereabouts of yer precious jewel ye can lay to it I could find it. Me and me crew have ways of persuadin' prisoners to talk. Ye would be drawin' us a map to help us locate it before we're finished wi' you. Ye do not know the value of the jewels on the *Isabella*. There's no reason I cannot have your jewel and the *Isabella*'s too.

Ye will lead me to it. And William? He will stay wi' me.

She said that with so much confidence that I lay with my fists clenched, fighting off the rush of hopelessness. I remembered her admiration of Queen Medb. "They would not give her what she wanted and she went to war to get it. I would." She had spoken surely. She spoke surely now. She wanted William and she would have him, whatever the consequences.

"Captain?"

"What is it, girl?"

"I know it troubles you that you cannot read...."

"I could if I wanted to. Why should I when I have others to read to me?"

"To be skilled at reading would be useful to you. I could teach you. Tonight I read from William Shakespeare and the words were so beautiful. In return for my lessons, with your good grace, you could allow..."

"Cod's breath, girl! One more word and I'll thrash ye right now."

I bit my lip, tasting blood.

I had played the only two cards I had and I had lost.

Perhaps I slept. My dreams woke me more than once,

dreams of the rat and the witch and islands, cold and barren. A dream of William, his smile, his voice. I dreamed of the time on the island when we had found love. I tried to recall the way my bones had softened when we held each other and all reality disappeared and I half-woke, filled with happiness and reluctant to come from the place my dreams had taken me.

Noise brought me fully awake.

Thumping on the cabin door, shouts, clamor on the deck above.

"We have the *Isabella* in our sights, Cap'n. Lookout spotted her, starboard."

The captain moved fast, pulling on clothes, unlocking the door.

I made to follow her and stopped, unsure. Was I to stay locked up?

But she was rushing, the door open behind her and I hurried after her onto the deck.

"The ship be's careened on the sand, just as you said, Cap'n," the quartermaster told her. He handed her the spyglass.

"Still careened? We are in time and in luck," Captain Moriarity said with a sidelong glance at Sebastian.

"Indeed, Cap'n." I did not detect much satisfaction in Sebastian's response.

There was much jostling and shoving at the starboard railings as the crew strained to see.

"Look at the sky, Cap'n," Sebastian said.

I looked, too.

A small black cloud hung directly above us, a smoky blot in the blue.

"I do not like it," Sebasian said. " 'Tis not too late to sail on past the *Isabella*. I fear…"

"Ye know I believe in luck," the captain said. "I believe in you. But I believe in meself too. That sky darkness be's only the remains of a storm cloud, blowed from somewhere. We will pay it no account."

I saw the glitter in her eyes, the frenzy. There was a pirate's greed in those eyes and the anticipation of a fight. There was also a hesitation. She was unsure. But to have this treasure within her grasp and to let go of it? I saw her jaw tighten.

"There are the other portents, and the black rat to deliberate on," Sebastian warned.

"I will hear no more." She examined the *Isabella* as the *Sea Wolf* sailed closer and still closer.

" Mr. Forrthinggale! William!" she called. "Get ye over here and give me a take on this."

It was to William that she first handed the spyglass.

"She is showing no colors," William said. " 'Tis mornin'

but there is no sign of life about her."

"Aye." She took the glass from William and gave it to the quartermaster. "What think ye, Mr. Forthinggale?"

He peered at the *Isabella*.

Around me I heard the mutterings of the crew and felt their apprehension. They had come this far and the riches of the *Isabella* were within their grasps. What did this strange first sighting signify?

"Has another ship come here afore us an' ransacked her?" someone asked. "Has another took her treasure?"

There was no answer from the captain or Mr. Forthinggale. They and William took turns with the spyglass as the distance between the two ships closed.

Beside me, a pirate with a ragged scar on his face fingered it and asked in a low voice, "Why does she consult the boy?"

"Because he be's hers, ye fool," someone answered.

His words were arrows, piercing me.

"Sebastian!" the captain called and Sebastian pushed beside her. "What do ye make o' this?"

He shook his head and did not take the spyglass she made to hand him. "I have no wish to look, Cap'n. May I speak with ye alone?"

Captain Moriarity gave a resigned sigh and moved away from the rest of the men.

Sebastian spoke to her earnestly but I saw her scowl. Her mind was set. I knew we would attack.

Sebastian spoke one more time with a raised and imploring voice: "We should turn around."

The captain whacked her cutlass against her leg. "Never," she said.

Those of the men, close enough to hear, gave a cheer.

"Go back like mangy dogs, wi' our tails a'tween our legs? There'll be none o' that." It was Claw doing the shouting.

"We be's afraid o' nothin'," Puce yelled. "Not wi' ye as our cap'n."

"We'll be ready to engage soon as ye give the order."

Captain Moriarity lifted one fist in the air. "'Tis settled then. We will go after her."

The pirate flag at the masthead had been hauled down and the English one raised. " 'Twill do no harm to look respectable," the captain said with a sly grin, leaning back to inspect it as it fluttered innocently against the sky. I saw her stiffen as she saw again the small black cloud that still hung motionless above us. "'Tis but a rain cloud," she muttered and Sebastian said, "Nothin' that easily explained, Cap'n."

Chapter Sixteen

Now we could see the *Isabella* clearly. New wood on her hull showed that she had been repaired but there was still caulking to be done and a gap to be attended to. She was a galleon with a long beak and a low forecastle. She had two decks and a square tuck stern. The name *Isabella* was written on her in gold. Boards and carpenter tools and barrels of what might be tar lay in the sand around her.

"She looks like she was disturbed as she was attending to her repairs," Mr. Forthinggale commented.

"Aye."

The ship lay on her side on the sand of the small cove

that was thick with trees and jungle undergrowth. Weak waves lapped around her hull.

"She's short on gunports," William said.

The captain grunted. "Guns take up cargo space. Those holds o' hers be's fat with gold and jewels just a'waitin' for us."

We were within hailing distance now.

"Ahoy the *Isabella*," the captain yelled through the bullhorn.

There was no answering hail.

"She be's a dead ship," someone said, and though it was a whisper it came clearly.

"Not dead, just sickly," another opined. "Weak and ready to be pillaged."

I did not consider myself superstitious. I thought I believed in luck but deemed it likely that it was a matter of knowing what you wanted and pursuing it no matter the obstacles. People said you were lucky. I thought plucky was perhaps a better word. But there had been such a lot of forebodings about this venture that it was difficult not to feel some trepidation. The black rat, the witch, the horseshoe, the Bonne Chance sign and now the isolated black cloud. Were they indeed warnings?

"Ahoy the *Isabella*," the captain called again. "We sail under the protection and power of the English crown."

It seemed our ship held its breath.

Again there was no response.

"Gunner! Send a shot across her, a friendly greetin' more'n a threat. We will see if that gets us an acknowledgment."

The quiet on the *Sea Wolf* was shattered by the loud boom of her cannon and the roar of the cannonball as it streaked through the air above the masts of the *Isabella*. Smoke rose in a trail that faded into the sky.

There was only silence from the galleon.

"Something is amiss," the captain said. "She has the look of an abandoned ship with no soul alive on her. But it could be a trap set for anyone that comes near. We have to play this wisely."

The men waited expectantly.

"Listen men!" she said. "We cannot get closer. We need more depth below our keel and we'd be grounded afore we got to her. 'Twould be a mistake to pound her from here. We want no damage to what we've come for." She paused, staring at the small beach, at the dense brush that grew thick around it, at the jutting cliffs, dark forbidding claws reaching out to the sea. "I have been informed, through me own sources, that on board that ship are religious artifacts, goblets of gold, crucifixes heavy with jewels, a Prie Dieu ornamented with better 'n a hundred gems."

I could hear the intake of breath from the men. This was even more than they had hoped for.

"We will sail beyond that point where we will not be sighted and we will wait for dark. Then we will launch the longboats and come upon her secretly, armed and ready. 'Tis better to go cautiously into the unknown."

" 'Tis a good plan," Mr. Forthinggale said, though the captain had not asked for his opinion. "We'll be on her deck afore she knows what's happenin'."

The men swarmed around Captain Moriarity, laughing and whooping.

After a minute she asked, "Sebastian, what will the weather be tonight?"

Sebastian fixed her with a steady gaze and for a heartbeat I thought he was going to refuse to answer. Or was he about to warn her again? But he only said, "I checked me string already. There will be a half moon but heavy clouds. If'n ye go through wi' this ye'll see little, but ye'll be little seen yerself."

The captain nodded.

"Navigator, set sail for yonder point. If we're bein' watched they'll be satisfied we sailed on and away. We will lie at ease till night comes."

There was a sudden yelp from somewhere in the crowd of men.

"Snake's britches!" Magruder shouted. "I just seen a rat, a black 'un, big as a cat. She was lookin' through the railings there like she was a person. Then she run down that hatch below decks."

"Ah, 'twas likely Catman's cat ye did see," Frenchy called. "Ye been lightheaded ever since the wench bit ye on the snout."

The captain looked quickly at Sebastian and away.

Chapter Seventeen

We were under sail heading for the point.

The captain and Mr. Forthinggale and the bosun, and those of us not engaged, watched the *Isabella* till we rounded the jutting cliff.

Nothing about her changed. Birds, brightly colored, swooped and skimmed across her. Looking through the spyglass the captain reported an iguana asleep in a corner of the deck.

"By heaven, the vessel looks deserted," she muttered. "'Twill be a sorrowful happening if she be's plundered already."

"Would there not be bodies? Dead men on the beach?"

Mr. Forthinggale asked.

"Perhaps. Unless they took time for the burials." The captain's brow was furrowed. "We could launch the boats and go straight for her now. But what if it is a ruse? Better we wait for dark."

"Aye," Mr. Forthinggale agreed.

The arms chest was unlocked again and weapons were distributed. Pistols and powder, two guns for every man. Ronan himself took possession of the grenades but the captain warned him. "We do not want to damage the booty aboard. Do not throw yer grenades less'n I give the order."

"Aye, aye, Cap'n."

Knives and cutlasses were sharpened.

The cook promised salmagundi and dried beef tongue to celebrate when all was finished but for now there was only hardtack to sustain us for whatever was to transpire. No one expected a strike from the *Isabella*, a ship so clearly incapacitated, but all safeguards aboard the *Sea Wolf* were checked and fortified.

Sebastian and I worked on the sail, so badly torn in the battle with the *Reprisal*. For once, he did not talk. But one time he muttered, as if to himself, "I fear this plan will end in the spillage of much blood," and he added, "but you and I will continue to stitch. We will need this topsail when what's left o' us voyage back to port."

Back to port, I thought as I stitched and watched the crew employ themselves and wait for dark. Will back to port be a new start for William and me? Will she let him go?

Night came. The half moon that Sebastian's string had predicted moved in and out of a sky filled with ominous gray clouds that hung like a pall over the sea. Among them I thought I could detect the darker darkness, lying in wait above our ship. But the captain was surely right. It had blown itself in from some place that had a storm.

Forty men were chosen to go.

One by one they touched the horseshoe on the main mast. Do they know that the luck was spilled out of it last night, I wondered? I thought not. Sebastian had righted it before it was remarked upon. The Bonne Chance board had been rehung so it was their belief that good fortune still sailed with them.

They spat in the ocean, spat in the eye of Davy Jones. "We's not goin' to ye yet, ye son of a black toad."

They tossed coins in the water as a tribute to Neptune.

O'Neill whistled and was shouted at. "Judas Ghost! Do ye want to bring misfortune down on us afore we gets our hands on the gold?"

There was edginess, expectation and shakiness in the

hands and voices of the men picked to go. But there was a cockiness, too. They were the ones deemed worthy by their captain.

The three longboats were lowered.

The men were armed and ready.

The captain was first to climb down the rope ladder, her two pistols hanging one at either end of her silk scarf, ready for her hands to reach. Silently she motioned for the others to join her. She had tied a dark kerchief about her head to hide the brightness of her hair that glowed even in the half dark. In the bow of the lead boat, she was a figurehead, a goddess, queen of the pirates. Sebastian was beside her. She had wanted him with her, and whatever his misgivings he had gone. She was his captain, and I suspected, the one person in the world he loved.

The others followed.

I breathed easier. At least William was not among them. Perhaps the captain had been unwilling to risk his life. Or perhaps she considered him inexperienced when every man in the boats was essential to the mission.

But then, I saw her beckon to William who stood by the railing. He was to be part of this after all. He moved. But before he could push his way to the ladder I rushed toward him.

"Don't go!" I clung to him, putting all the conviction I

was capable of into my voice. "There will be death. Sebastian says. Do not let her take you."

Hands pulled me away from him, rough hands that tore at my shirt and shoulders.

"Yez holdin' them up down below," someone grunted.

"Have ye no shame, ye hussy?"

"Let go of me." I squirmed and bit and clawed.

Then William's arms were around me and he whispered, "I have to do what she asks. It is for us. Do not fret, me love. I will stay safe."

From the lead boat came the hoarse whisper, "Time's a'wastin'. Get ye down here, William. Yer place is wi' me. Stand back girl or I'll order ye locked away."

Against my hair William whispered. "Ye are me heart."

My hands reached out to hold him back, but he was gone.

"Ye are me heart." How had I ever doubted his love? But now he was going into danger. To myself I repeated the captain's prayer. "Keep him safe."

I watched him climb into the second boat.

He did not glance up.

The sea was calm. The boats drifted gently, jerking a little on their ropes, as anxious to go as the pirates they carried.

On soundless oars they pulled away.

The rest of the crew that were still aboard the *Sea Wolf* hung over the railing till the boats were out of sight. All was silence and darkness except when the moon came out of the clouds to shiver on the sea.

Some of the men padded quietly along the deck. There was a half-hidden anxiety, a straining to know what was happening, a frustration at not being able to see around the point, to set eyes on the prize and their comrades.

The quartermaster, who had been left on board in charge of the *Sea Wolf*, was stopped as he walked the deck, stopped by murmured questions that he could not answer.

Each time I saw a shadow race along the deck I thought it was the black rat and I skittered away from it. It never was. Once my foot touched an old canvas shoe abandoned in a corner and I stifled a scream. A shoe was not a rat. There was no doubt in my mind that there was a rat down there, lurking below decks and that it might come up. But whether or not it was a witch or an omen of death I did not know.

I smelled salmagundi cooking and the smell of it, usually delicious, roiled my stomach. I tried to take comfort in the knowledge that Cook was already making it in preparation for the celebration. It seemed like a good omen in a ship of omens. Over and over again I thought on William's last words to me. Not a share of a ship or the needs of its indomitable captain could persuade him. In spite of the danger the remembrance of his words made my blood sing. He would come back to me. I allowed myself to dream.

And then the night burst open with noise, the terrible hiss of cannonballs roaring through the air, the sharp crackle of gunfire, the screams of men in agony. Flashes of blinding light lit up the dark clouds.

On the *Sea Wolf* there was a stunned silence followed by commotion.

"What's happenin'?"

"That's cannon fire."

"Cod's breath, they be's attackin' our boats! 'Tis not us attackin' them."

"They waited for us. They knowed all along that we was here," the quartermaster shouted. "They're blowin' our boats out o' the water."

"Turn our ship about," Finnegan shouted. "We cannot leave them to perish."

The quartermaster stood as if undecided.

"What's keepin' ye, Quarter? Can't ye hear what's occurrin'?"

It was as though the quartermaster came awake then. Had he been taking time to consider... to consider maybe leaving them, taking the *Sea Wolf* and fleeing?

"Hurry!" I screamed. "Hurry!"

"We'll not be able to get close," he said at last. "Ye heard Cap'n. The sea be's too shallow."

"We can get closer than here," someone yelled. No need for quiet now. All was disorder.

There was the creak of the rope as the anchor was pulled. The men rushed to raise the sails. Slowly the *Sea Wolf* came about.

I could barely breathe. William! In the midst of that? My William? Hurt? Shot? Blown apart?

I ran to the bow, leaning over to lie against the bowsprit, hastening her on. Hurry! Hurry! It was all I could do to stop myself from jumping into the sea and swimming to where the guns blasted. But what could I do, even if I made it that far? I made a promise to Neptune. Let William live and I will do whatever you ask of me. Even give him up.

But not that. Please, not that.

The pandemonium, the boom of musket and roar of cannon, seemed to tear the sky. I looked up. Unharmed, the cloud still hung above the *Sea Wolf*.

Slowly, slowly our bowsprit rounded the point. Behind me was a shouted command. "This is far as we can go! Drop anchor."

The ship shuddered to a stop.

Now I could see through the murk of gun smoke, but I could not bear to see. Someone wailed and I think it was me.

On the dark sea two of the longboats lay, torn apart, ripped from stem to stern. Bodies were strewn around them, some motionless, some swimming or struggling to reach the one boat that remained and was drifting away from them.

Cannonballs slammed the water. The noses of guns sprouted from the underbrush behind the *Isabella*. I knew immediately what had happened. They had spotted the *Sea Wolf* earlier, moved their cannon into cover and waited for us to attack the way a mongoose lay in wait for a snake. Small-arms fire splattered, like deadly rain, around the men in the water. There were screams, moans loud enough to be heard, voices raised in panic.

Oh where was William? Was he one of those, floating facedown, or was he that one, missing a leg, floating in a pool of oily water.

I snatched the spyglass from the quartermaster's hand, ignoring his order to hand it back, pushing him away when he tried to grab it.

Where is that golden hair?

Please, let me find him among all the others.

I could not see him.

And then I did.

It was not the gold of his hair that helped me spot him because his hair was dark with seawater and perhaps blood, I could not tell. It was my heart that led me to him, that found him for me among all the other struggling bodies.

He was on his stomach but moving, one arm flailing, the other dragging at his side.

"William," I shouted and even as I called his name he slipped under the water.

Without another thought I climbed onto the railing, aware of the shouts of the crew, of the quartermaster screaming, "What are ye doin,' ye heedless girl," aware of his voice fading as I jumped and the sea swallowed me, dragging me down and down and down.

Chapter Eighteen

*T*he sea was cold, so cold.

Something was pulling at me, trying to keep me down, some creature, but it was not Davy Jones, it was my green pantaloons, filled with water. I wanted to kick them off but the movement was too difficult.

My chest was ready to explode.

My ears thumped.

I knew I was drowning.

But I wasn't. I was up, up into the blessed air, taking deep gulps of it, feeling it burn my chest, my body sinking a little, coming back.

Around me were feeble shouts, voices calling for help.

Shots dimpled the water. The whine of them was like some strange insect. I saw Puce and made to touch him and saw that he was dead, his eyes still open and staring.

William, oh William! Don't die. I am here.

I tried to recreate where I had seen him when I searched from the deck. Over that way, over to the side. He had been making for the empty boat.

And then I saw him but he seemed so far away, across bodies, across broken pieces of the longboats, across the churned-up sea.

I took hold of a piece of planking and tried to lie across it but it was small and sank under me.

I found it again, held it in front of me and began to kick.

Hold on, William! I am coming!

I tried to strike out but the water felt cushiony, like a feather bed inviting me to rest, to allow it to comfort me. My strength was going. An oar floated ahead of me but I never seemed to reach it. I should just let go.

Someone was splashing beside me. A hand grabbed my arm.

I had a surge of energy. This person was holding on to me and he was going to pull me under. "Stop it!" I hissed. "Stop it!"

Then I heard his mumbled words.

"Keep movin'," he spluttered. It was Frenchy, whose green pantaloons I was wearing.

Then I saw William.

I tried to free myself from Frenchy, plunging toward my love. Frenchy let go of me, grabbed William with one hand, and struggled with the other to reach the gunwale of the floating boat.

I had renewed hope and with it a little of my strength returned.

I held William's head above water, lunged toward the boat and caught hold of the gunwale, hanging on to it, hanging on to William. Was he still alive? I could not tell.

Frenchy was behind us, taking William's weight.

I heaved and Frenchy heaved and we grunted and pushed, William a sodden weight between us. He was in the boat.

I tried to climb in after him but I was too tired and worn and Frenchy caught my legs in the water-heavy pantaloons and raised me up to tumble over beside William.

Now Frenchy was trying to pull himself in and I made myself crawl and reach over and grab the neck of his canvas shirt and haul him up.

The three of us lay like wet sacks of grain in the bottom of the boat.

"William," I whispered and I forced myself up to crawl to him. "He's full of water," I said. "Frenchy, help me turn him over."

Between us we rolled him onto his stomach.

Water spewed from his mouth. He was coughing, and my heart rejoiced. He was alive! Relief warmed me through the chill of my dripping clothes.

He turned his head. "Catherine!"

"Be still, my love. You are hurt. Try not to move."

Frenchy lifted William's limp arm. " 'Tis his shoulder. I don't think it be's broke," he said. "But 'tis pulled out o' place."

"Catherine? How come ye... William's voice was weak.

"I came after you. Do not worry about that now."

The gunfire was less. The cannon roar had ceased. There was a dangerous, nerve-racking quietness in the sea around us. Bodies floated, dark shapes in the water.

"We must check," I said. "Some may still be alive."

"I think them that is are makin' for that spit o' land yonder. The one we come around. Cap'n be's safe," Frenchy said. "I see her, standin' there on the shore."

I looked where he pointed and saw the shadows of the men, some already on the strip of sand, some still struggling toward it. I saw the captain, taller and more upright than any of them. And beside her I saw a small figure, childlike. Sebastian? I blinked, the better to clear my eyes from the stinging of the salt. Yes. The captain and Sebastian.

It gladdened me to see Sebastian, safe from the guns and the sea. And Captain Moriarity? Yes, I would not have wished her to perish. Had it not been for her love of William we might have been comrades, the both of us daughters of sea captains. But she wanted William. She fought for him. Could I blame her?

"They'll head for the point where the *Sea Wolf* lies," Frenchy said.

I nodded. "But we must look if there are others in need of our help."

There were only three oars in the oarlocks.

"I saw one, floating," I said. "I still see it. If we can paddle over there I can reach it."

I fished it out of the water.

Frenchy and I took the oars, telling William that a one-armed rower would be more hindrance than help.

"You would be pullin' us around in circles," Frenchy said. "Sit ye back."

We rowed among the floating bodies. One, who at first appeared to be dead, reached weakly for the oar we held out to him but as we pulled on it he let go and fell back into the water. When we stretched out to grab him we could see that he had used his last effort and had no life left in him. He was Flanagan who was of Ireland and would never see it again. We saw Ronan. He was alive still. We dragged him in with us and he sprawled at our feet, gulping in air.

Half-hearted gunfire splashed around us. One bullet tore splinters from the side of our boat.

We threaded between bodies and debris, calling out, touching. We found none other to save.

"No use lookin' more," Frenchy said. "We have to row ourselves out of range."

We leaned on the oars and I closed my eyes and silently prayed for the souls of the dead. I opened them when William said, "Look at the rat! 'Tis a giant one. It looks like it came off the *Sea Wolf*. I never saw one as big or as black."

"Witch," I whispered but neither William or Frenchy or Ronan seemed to hear.

I watched the rat swim for the shore where the *Isabella* lay. I told myself it was just a rat. Nothing more. Going for a change of ship now that its job on the *Sea Wolf* was done. HER job?

"The *Isabella* be's tired o' the fightin'," William said. "They knows they won and their treasure is safe."

I knelt beside him. "Are you in pain?"

"'Tis not much." He smiled and even now, even in this horror of a night, that smile made everything better. "Thank ye for coming for me, Catherine."

"I would always come for you," I said and lightly kissed his salt-caked lips.

"Frenchy?" I touched his arm. "Frenchy? We thank you for what you did this night."

"Aye."

How strange, I thought. I wore his trousers, I saw him and heard his name spoken, but I never knew him. Now he had helped save us. He was a pirate who I'd thought cared for nothing but gold and treasure. But in him was some measure of honor.

"Frenchy," I said, "you could row yourself across and join your old crew, if you have a mind to. Captain Moriarity would be glad to have you back. Though William and I would be obliged if you helped us to shore first. We want to escape, if that's not too strong a word."

I turned to look once again at the far-off shadow shape of the captain and Sebastian. Had we escaped? Would she let us—let William—go?

Then I remembered her face when she spoke of the *Sea Wolf*, of her joy and pride in her ship. She would never forsake it.

"I understand, Mistress Catherine. I'll not be goin'

back neither," Frenchy said. "Me time wi' the *Sea Wolf* is past. I'm an adventure-seekin' man and there're other adventures ahead. I'll tell ye true, I could use a change o' captain, too. Don't ye be worryin' about Ronan. I've seen men that's out o' their heads afore, and they've come back. I'll see to him."

"It's good of you," I said.

Frenchy's grin showed his small white teeth. "We be's maties, Ronan an' me. Ye've heard o' honor among pirates? There's not too much o' it but there's some."

I leaned over and touched Ronan's arm. "Ronan? Frenchy's going to look after you."

He did not answer or move, but perhaps he heard.

The three of us stared about us at the heaving water and the dead that floated on it.

"Sebastian saw all this before it transpired," I whispered. "He warned the captain."

Frenchy shrugged. "'Twould have been a struggle between her superstition and her greed. And her duty to her crew," he added.

"Yes."

I sighed, then bent down and wrung the water out of my pantaloons and the tails of my shirt.

"Is that yer flute?" William asked.

"Aye," I ran my fingers across it where I had thrust it,

tight in the waist of my trousers.

"I fear I lost yer mother's petticoat." William coughed a gurgly cough. "Half the Caribbean is still inside of me," he said, wiping his mouth. "I'm sorry about the petticoat."

" 'Tis nothing," I said, although it was. "You can buy me another, just like it."

His gaze made me tremble.

"It's a hard pull to shore," he told Frenchy. "I'm sorry I'm of no use to ye."

"Rest," I said. "Frenchy and I can do it."

"Cap'n showed me the charts for hereabouts," William told us. "The land is an island, but a big 'un. There will be game and water and fruit." He laid his hand over mine, wincing at the pain as he moved. " 'Twill not be like Pox Island, me love. There be's a settlement on the other side and we'll make for that. Ships'll come. Ships to take us home. Will you and Ronan stay wi' us?"

Frenchy leaned on the oar. "I will come wi' ye as far as the shore. I'll find help for Ronan if he's still in need of it. After that I'll be on me way, Ronan. I likes to be on me own."

"What will you do?" I asked.

"There will be another vessel for me. 'Twill be another pirate ship, sailin' on new waters. Pirating is all I know."

I was shivering and William reached over and cautiously drew me close. I hugged him gently, and then picked up the oars.

We will survive, I thought, as Frenchy and I pulled toward the shore. We will make our way back to Port Teresa and we will have the life we planned in the despairing closeness of Pox Island. We will build our own ship or perhaps we will live in my dear old home and have two little goats like Daisy and Pansy. I will go with William to my mother's grave on Cobb Hill and I will stand at her resting place and play for her the song she loved. I will tell her of my father and how he died, protecting me. As time passes my fear of islands will fade, as the smell of gun smoke is fading now.

The bulk of the *Isabella* lay asleep in the sand, a snake, satisfied with its kill, ready if another thief should come to steal her treasure. That is the way it is with pirates. I had always thought I wanted to be one, but then I was young and untried and ignorant. I am still young, but I have learned what I want in life and it is not this.

I shook my head to clear it of old thoughts and pulled on the oars, pulling away from the past, rowing, with William beside me, into our future.

Eve Bunting grew up in Ireland—a country of storytellers—and came to California in 1958 with her husband and three small children. Her first book, an Irish folktale, was published in 1972. Since then she has written more than 250 books for children of all ages, from picture books to young adult novels, as well as non-fiction. She enjoys writing all types of stories for young readers, including those that address social issues.

Eve Bunting's books have won many awards and honors over the years, including the Golden Kite award from the Society of Children's Book Writers and Illustrators, the Edgar from the Mystery Writers of America, and awards from twenty-seven states voted on by children. She is a two-time winner of the California Young Reader Medal. In 2006 she won the first Arab American Book Award for One Green Apple, illustrated by Ted Lewin. Eve Bunting and her husband live in Pasadena, California. They now have six grandchildren.